Road Kill

D1522469

Kristen Middleton

Other Books By Author

Night Roamers Series (In order)-
Blur
Shiver
Vengeance
Illusions

Venom Series (In order)-
Venom
Slade
Toxic

Enchanted Series (In order)-
Enchanted Secrets
Enchanted Objects
Enchanted Spells

Planet Z (Stand Alone)

Zombie Games Series (In order)-
Origins
Running Wild
Dead Endz

Road Kill
End Zone

Kristen
MIDDLETON
Fantasy, Horror, and Romance.

As always,
Thank you to my family
and friends
for their support
and patience

And thank you, God, for the many blessings in
my life.

PROLOGUE

He waited anxiously in the crook of the tree, wondering how he'd escape the three zombies lingering down below. He was pretty sure they were aware of him; in fact, he was positive they could smell him from the way they continued to sniff the air while making those nasty, gurgling noises.

I have to get out of here.

Rubbing the sweat from his brow, he decided it was time. There was no way he could wait any longer. It had been at least two or three hours since he'd left Allie and Kylie, and they were probably freaking out, thinking he'd totally abandoned them. In a few hours the sun would be down and it would be harder to find his way back through the woods. Now, he'd have to return with his tail between his legs, knowing he hadn't accomplished anything but hiding out in a tree like a scared little wuss.

I may just as well have the word 'fail' embedded in my forehead, he thought. *What a waste of time.*

Releasing a sigh, he reached into his jeans and took out the pink rubber ball he'd found the day before at the rest-stop. It was a longshot, but he had to cause a distraction and hope the zombies moved away to investigate. More than likely, however, they were just far too stupid and would completely ignore it. As he raised the ball to throw it into the woods, a movement in the woods caught his attention.

A pig!

The young Yorkshire was snorting happily as he stopped and began eating something on the grass which, honestly, looked like cheesy-rice or puke.

Luke shuddered as the zombies moved toward the pig, hoping that Wilbur was enjoying his last meal.

With his heart pounding, he waited until the creatures were about twenty feet away from his position and only then did he begin to descend the tree. Just as he was about to reach the bottom, however, the entire tree began to tremble and shake. Stunned, he jumped to the ground, which also rumbled under his tennis shoes.

An earthquake?

Frightened and worried that the earth was going to open up and swallow him whole, he ran back toward the dairy farm. It was the last place he'd left the girls and he hoped they were still okay.

1

"I can't take it anymore," groaned Nora. "If I have to listen to one more song by 'Wailing Jennings', I'm going to shoot myself in the head."

"It's '*Waylon* Jennings'," corrected Henry, "and you need to show him a little respect, God rest his soul. Jesus, I had to listen to 'Shityeah' and lost two hours of my life that an old-timer like me can't afford to waste."

"It's '*Hellyeah*', and they freaken' *rock*," said Nora.

"Rock? Sounds like the main singer had something stuck in his throat," said Henry. "It's amazin' what you kids listen to these days. Why, back in the day –"

Nora rolled her eyes. "Oh, here we go…"

"Artists like Elvis Presley and Chuck Berry knew how to entertain their fans."

"Well, even I can appreciate Elvis, so why don't you just stop while you're ahead," said Nora.

He went on. "That there Elvis, by golly, he made the women-folk crazy with his gyratin' hips and velvety, smooth voice. I remember this gal I dated in my early twenties, Barbara Jean Crawford, she got so worked up listening to Elvis on the radio on the way to dinner during our second date, that she jumped my bones right there in the parking lot of the restaurant. I saved myself five dollars that night, man, 'cause," he cackled, "we never made that reservation."

"Oh, for the love of God," sighed Nora.

"I purchased every one of his records after that and always kept an eight-track in my truck, just in case I was feeling a little frisky."

"Wow, you, frisky? That's odd."

"Yep, went through a lot of shocks in those days, but," he smiled, wistfully, "them were some mighty good times."

"Okay, we're even," said Nora.

"What do you mean?" he asked.

"I just lost minutes of my life that I'll never get back, either."

Having heard enough, I sat up and stretched my arms. "Where are we?"

"Oh, look who's finally woken up from the dead," replied Henry, glancing back at me in the rearview mirror. "I'm surprised *Shityeah* didn't scare you awake, Wild."

"Hellyeah," grunted Nora.

"Nope. I must have really needed the rest," I yawned. "I didn't wake up until I heard you two bickering."

"I'm surprised you could even sleep through this twisted country twang," said Nora.

Honestly, I wasn't that crazy about it either, at least not the older country music, but when I saw the look Henry gave her, I changed the subject. "Nora, did you happen to find any of your dad's CDs?"

She began fiddling with the black leather wristband that Billie had given her. "Yeah."

"Why don't you pop one in?" I asked.

"Later," she replied.

After only a few hours on the road, we'd found a music shop and had stocked up on some CDs for the ride back to Minnesota.

"Your dad's a musician?" asked Henry.

Nora stared out her side window. "Yep, he's the lead vocalist for Death Row."

Henry scratched his whiskers. "Death Row? Sounds like one of those heavy-metal bands. Your dad doesn't bite off the heads of bats or urinate on his fans, does he?"

Nora turned to him and scowled. "No, but he does smoke too much, tell tall tales, and thinks he's God's gift to women. Like someone else we all know."

Henry was silent for a minute and then his face turned red. "You talkin' about me? I'll have you know that I've never told a lie. I've had me a life filled with experiences that would knock your socks off, young lady. In fact, if I don't survive this zombie apocalypse mumbo jumbo, I don't want anyone feeling sorry for me. I've had no regrets in life, and as far as I'm concerned, every day from here on out is a gift from the man above."

"Oh, stop talking about death, old man. You'll probably outlive every damn one of us," said Nora.

He reached into his pocket and pulled out a tin of chew. "Not if I can help it. Why do you think I decided to tag along with the two of you? It wasn't because it sounded like a fine plan. Hell no, I'm here because someone's got to keep you reckless young girls from getting yourselves killed. But, I tell you what – if I die because of it, I know in this here ticker," he said, pointing to his chest, "that it certainly won't be in vain."

I reached forward and gently patted his shoulder. "Come on now, Henry, we're not going to let that happen. *None* of us are going to die on this trip."

"Speaking of which, I think we should focus on getting gas right now," said Nora, motioning toward the gas gauge. "Before this *van* dies."

"Damn these gas-guzzling-mommy-mobiles," he muttered.

"It's still better than that gas-hog we left Atlanta in," I said.

We'd been on the road now for two days and were somewhere in Illinois. After almost running out of gas the day before, we'd traded the truck in for an abandoned Honda Odyssey, because Henry said it would have better gas mileage.

Henry looked at the fuel level and frowned. "I hope we can find something soon. You said you know how to siphon gas, Nora?"

"Yeah," she said, pulling her dark hair up into a ponytail. I stared at the blue fairy tattooed on the back of her neck and wished I would have gotten something before everything had gone to hell. My dad, who was pretty old-fashioned, would have never allowed it, however.

"So, how did you learn to siphon gas?" I asked.

"Don't ask," she answered with a smirk.

"There's another town coming up, about ten miles," said Henry. "Let's just hope the zombie situation is manageable."

"We need more food, too," said Nora, slipping a piece of spearmint gum into her mouth. "I'm freaken' hungry and gum just isn't doing it anymore."

"I'm hungry, too," I said.

She handed me a piece of gum.

We drove the rest of the way in silence as I stared at my engagement ring, wondering what Bryce was doing at that particular moment. More than likely, he'd thrown quite the fit after reading my note and was probably debating on whether or not to track me down. Although I had to agree that it had been a reckless decision on my part, I still stood firm on it; my grandparents' as well as Nora's dad's lives were at stake. *If* they were still alive, I had to go back for them. Besides, if I could survive the nightmare back in Atlanta, this would be a piece of cake.

"Heads up, girls, the town of Baylor is coming up," said Henry.

I stared out the window as we entered the rundown little town. Just like most of the other places we'd passed through, it was empty and barren, except for the familiar sight of the dead that shuffled in and out of broken entryways or around street corners.

"Gross," groaned Nora, rolling up her window.

Yes, the stench of death and decay greeted us like old friends. Baylor, however, held a little something extra for us.

"Crap," I pointed up the street. "Check it out."

"Oh, my God, are those nuns?" gasped Nora.

I watched in wonder as three women, all cloaked in black habits and yielding sharp weapons, stood outside of an old drugstore, fending off a group of overzealous zombies.

"Hurry, pull up to them," I said, picking up the ax I'd set down by my feet.

"Already ahead of you," said Henry, picking up speed as he steered toward the group.

When we stopped, Nora and I both got out and advanced on the zombies that were threatening the women. Fortunately, they were so transfixed on the nuns that they didn't pay any notice of us until it was too late.

I moved behind a tall, gangly walker, whose head was bent at an unusual angle, and swung the ax with everything I had. As it fell to its knees, I dislodged my weapon from its skull and kicked the limp torso to the cement.

"Watch out, child!" hollered one of the nuns, a heavier-set woman with red curls poking out of her hood.

"I got it," said Nora, delivering a roundhouse kick to the zombie rushing toward me. It fell to the ground and she quickly finished it off with her newest bludgeoning device – a long wrench we'd picked up in the last town. I cringed at the horrible crunching noise it made as she slammed it into the zombie's skull.

"Thanks," I said.

From there, I beheaded two additional zombies while Nora experimented with different ways of using her new weapon, delighting mostly in the "ram and twist" method. When we'd finished off the rest of the zombies, the nuns thanked us profusely.

"Thank goodness, you showed up," said the red-haired nun. "I don't know about Sister Theresa or Sister Elizabeth, but I'm not sure if I could have really attacked one of them." She held up her large butcher knife. "The thought just sickens me."

"Well, you have to destroy them," said Nora, kicking at one of the zombies on the ground as it made one last feeble attempt to reach for her, "if you want to survive."

Henry, who'd gotten out of the truck, took off his Stetson and nodded. "She's right. Don't you burden yourself with the guilt of saving your own life; I'm sure God would understand."

The nun looked at the bloody carnage we'd created and shook her head. "Well, I'm not so sure about that."

"Why?" I asked, curious to know the nun's take on the zombies and all of the bloodshed. "What do you mean?"

The nun turned to me and smiled grimly. "Because these *are* the '*End of Days*', honey. These walking corpses are all part of God's plan to eliminate the evil and corrupt, to cleanse the earth, so that we can start fresh."

Henry's eyes widened. "Uh, excuse me? You mean…"

"Yes," said the other nun. "This is just the preliminary to what's going to happen next."

"You mean you seriously think it's going to get worse than this?" I asked, not knowing what to believe.

"Yes, child, *much* worse," she replied, laying a hand on my shoulder.

2

"Wake up, Allie," whispered Kylie, shaking her shoulder.

"What?" she mumbled, opening her eyes. "More tremors?"

"No, if there'd have been another quake, you'd have woken up with me screaming my butt off. It's just…" she sighed. "Luke's not back yet."

Allie pushed herself up. "How long has it been?"

"Well, you've been asleep for at least two hours."

She groaned. *That meant he'd been gone for four or five hours, maybe longer.*

"Do you think they got him?" whispered Kylie, biting her lower lip.

"I don't know," said Allie, pulling out pieces of straw from her blonde hair. "Probably not. He's pretty smart, so I don't think he would have let that happen."

"Yeah, but if he was outnumbered..."

"Don't say that, I'm sure he's fine." Allie wrinkled her nose. "Oh man, it stinks in here. Like a mixture of horse manure and..."

"Death," replied Kylie.

They were hiding up in the loft of an old barn in the middle of nowhere, while a dozen or so zombies wandered aimlessly below, sniffing the air, searching for the source of the succulent smell of living flesh floating somewhere in the air.

"We should have stayed in the van," said Kylie, playing with a piece of straw. She twirled it between her fingers and then flicked it away. "How are we ever going to get out of here?"

"Don't worry. Luke will be back and he'll know what to do."

"Let's hope," sighed Kylie.

They'd run out of gas less than twenty-four hours after leaving Atlanta, and had been forced to abandon the van on the side of the road. After walking a couple of miles, they'd chanced upon an old farmhouse, inhabited by the stench of rotten food and even rottener… zombies. Tired and hungry, they'd dashed to the barn to hide up in the loft while Luke went in search of another vehicle for the three of them.

"I don't know, I still don't think he should have left us," said Kylie. "It's too dangerous to be alone out there. We could have helped him."

"Or we could have been eaten," said Allie. "Look, it'll be easier for him if he doesn't have to worry about us."

"Yeah, I suppose," she said.

Allie crawled over to the edge of the loft and looked down into the lower part of the barn. "None of them have tried using the ladder?"

Kylie moved along next to her. "They couldn't figure it out," she said as they watched the zombies shuffle around, moaning and slightly agitated. "One of them stood at the bottom, looking up, and I thought for sure, he was going to crawl up here, but fortunately for us, he was just too dense to figure out how to do it."

"Thank God."

One of the zombies, a woman with long stringy hair and a chewed-up nose, must have heard something, because she looked up at them and began growling. Then, two other zombies joined in, and soon the entire barn sounded like a bunch of cats in heat.

The girls backed away from the edge.

"God, I wish they'd just stop," groaned Allie, holding her hands over her ears.

Kylie closed her eyes and began praying.

"What are you doing?" asked Allie.

Kylie opened her eyes. "Praying that someone will come and save us."

Allie closed her eyes and began praying, too. Anything was worth trying at this point.

After several minutes of praying, both girls noticed the zombies had quieted down and they opened their eyes.

"*No* way," whispered Allie, peeking over the edge of the loft again.

Not only had the zombies quieted down, but they'd actually left the barn.

"Don't get too excited," said Kylie, walking over to the open window. She leaned down and pointed. "Look."

Allie stared in horror at the scene outside. Luke had returned and was holding some kind of makeshift torch, trying to get back into the barn, while a crowd of about fifteen zombies were moving toward him.

"He needs our help!" cried Allie, rushing toward the ladder.

"Are you kidding me? There's too many!" hollered Kylie, grabbing her arm. "It's suicide to go down there. We lost our weapons and there's no way we can kill those things with our bare hands."

The sound of gunfire startled both of them and they dashed back over to the window. A big red pickup was now parked outside of the barn, its owner firing his gun at the zombies surrounding Luke.

"Holy cow," whispered Allie, staring at the tall, muscular guy. "That guy is fine."

"Seriously, he's like, old," said Kylie. "He has to be in his twenties."

Noticing the two girls looking down from the window, Luke ran into the barn and yelled for them to climb down the ladder. When they reached the bottom, they both hugged him and his face turned crimson.

"Oh, my God, are you okay?" cried Allie, noticing the way he winced when she released him.

"Yeah, I'm okay. I had a close call with a zombie earlier. Thankfully, the lower part of his face was missing and he couldn't bite me." He shuddered. "I don't think I've ever smelled anything that bad in my life."

"You weren't trapped in the barn with us and a group of those things, these last few hours. Even the cow dung couldn't mask the smell," said Kylie.

The gunfire ceased suddenly, and the three of them stepped outside of the barn to see what was happening.

"Do you know that guy?" whispered Kylie as the stranger walked toward them.

"No," he said, stomping out the flames on the torch. "I never did find help. At least, not before this guy showed up."

"Hopefully he *is* help," whispered Allie. "Or at the very least, friendly."

The guy didn't appear very friendly; in fact, as he stepped closer, he looked more ominous than anything.

"Stay close to me," said Luke.

"He looks like some kind of a biker dude," whispered Allie. She smiled. "That's kind of hot."

"Oh, my God," snorted Kylie.

"Hey," called the man, stopping a few yards away. He had a flattened blonde Mohawk, a couple piercings on his stubbly face, and some kind of tribal tattoo on his left arm. "So, are you kids okay?"

"Yes," said Luke, stepping in front of the girls. "Um, thanks for helping with those things."

He stared at Luke for a minute and then shook his head. "You'd have been a real goner if I wouldn't have seen you. Don't you have any kind of weapons?"

"Yeah, had a gun, but I ran out of bullets," said Luke. "Have a knife, too, but I thought that maybe the fire would keep them at bay."

"They're not animals. And they're obviously not afraid of fire."

"I guess not," said Luke.

The man stepped closer, slipping his revolver into the back waistband of his faded jeans. "You girls okay?"

Allie moved around Luke, to get a better look at him and noticed he was even younger than she'd originally thought. "We're fine. What's your name?" she asked.

He stared at her for a minute and then answered, "Justice."

Kylie raised her eyebrows. "Justice?"

He looked away. "My mom, she was into old westerns."

Allie smiled. "How old are you?"

He cocked an eyebrow. "Why?"

Her cheeks turned pink. "Just wondering."

"Twenty," said Justice. "So, you three out here alone?"

Luke stepped around Allie, pushing her back behind him. "There *are* more of us. We've just been separated temporarily."

"Good," said Justice. "Try to *un-separate*, as soon as you can. It's too dangerous to be out here on your own. Especially for you kids." He then turned around and began walking away.

"Wait!" hollered Kylie, catching up to him. "So, um, where are you going?"

He shrugged. "Was going to check the house for food or other supplies. You guys get a chance to do that yet?"

"Not really," said Kylie. "There were zombies in there when we showed up. Probably still is."

"Well, at this point, I'm hungrier than they are," he said, walking toward his truck. He reached into the back and pulled out a machete. "So, they'd better stay out of my way in the kitchen. Here," he said, reaching into the truck a second time. He picked up an old wooden baseball bat and held it out to Luke. "Use this if you have to."

"Thanks," he replied.

Justice nodded and started walking toward the house, machete raised. "Stay outside," he ordered, "until I give you the okay to come in."

"You want any help?" asked Luke.

"I got this," he replied, raising his hand in the air. "Just stay out of the way."

They watched as Justice climbed the stairs to the porch, opened the screen door, and disappeared inside.

"Think he'll be okay in there?" asked Kylie.

"Did you see him? It's obvious he knows what he's doing," replied Allie.

A few minutes later, Kylie's question was answered. Justice stepped back outside, the blade of his machete covered in red and black slime.

He held the door open and waved. "Well, come on in, then, if you're hungry. Lucky for us, I found some food in the pantry, still edible."

"Are they all dead?" asked Kylie.

"Yeah, there were only four left in the house. Watch where you step, though, it's a little messy inside."

They walked past him and into the farmhouse, stopping abruptly as they encountered two headless zombies sprawled out on the wooden floor.

"Oh," croaked Allie. "It smells rancid in here."

"It helps if you breathe through your mouth," said Justice, moving around her.

"No, it doesn't help," she said, following him into the kitchen. "Not when it's this bad."

"Um, you know, I'm not really hungry anymore," mumbled Kylie as she stepped over a wet, mangled eyeball.

"Yes, you are. Come on, you have to eat something," said Luke. "We all do."

Fortunately, the kitchen was free of zombies and didn't smell quite as bad as the rest of the house.

"Here's the pantry," said Justice, opening up a door on the other side of the kitchen. "Check all this out."

"Oh, my God!" squealed Allie, picking up a box of Cocoa Pops. She turned to Kylie. "Didn't this used to be your favorite cereal?"

"Yeah. I guess this farm didn't care about added sugar and artificial flavoring," joked Kylie. "Looks like they've got Pop-Tarts, too."

"Oh, I love those," moaned Allie, grabbing the box from her.

"And that's not all," said Justice, lifting up a jug of apple juice. "Don't know about you guys, but this is the closest I've come to real fruit in a long time."

"Nice," said Allie, biting into a Pop-Tart. "Mm… this is so good."

"Wow, look at all of this stuff… cans of tuna and chicken," said Luke, pulling them off of the shelf. "Peanuts and pretzels. We hit the mother-load."

"Fortunately for us, this house must be one of the few places around here that hasn't been looted yet. Let's put everything on the counter," said Justice. "Then we'll sort it all out and go from there."

They cleaned out the pantry, pulling out boxes of graham crackers, canned veggies and soup, and more boxes of cereal.

"Here's a can opener," said Luke, pulling it out of a drawer. "I call dibs on the Spaghetti-O's."

"Eat sparingly," said Justice. "All of you. Obviously, you're going to need to save some for later. Plus, if it's been a while since you've eaten, you might not feel all that well if you gorge yourself."

Although they were all hungry, and it had been a while since they'd eaten anything besides chips, they all agreed that the food needed to be rationed.

"It's hard to find food now," said Justice, filling a small glass of apple juice. "Other survivors are raiding homes and stores, hoarding everything. I haven't eaten anything in two days."

"So, are you all alone?" asked Allie.

"Yep," he said, raising the glass to his lips.

"Where are you heading?" asked Luke.

He shrugged. "Nowhere in particular. Just trying to survive, man."

"You can come with us," said Allie, her eyes lighting up. "We're going to Minnesota, to find my sister."

"Oh yeah? You sure she's even alive?"

She nodded. "My sister and Nora are bad-asses. They're both alive."

Justice leaned against the counter and smiled. "Oh, is that right?"

Allie nodded solemnly. "Cassie has a Black Belt in karate and has killed *hundreds* of zombies already. If anyone is still alive, it's her."

"A badass-martial–arts zombie killer, huh? Well, although I wouldn't mind meeting your sister or her friend, gas is getting harder to come by these days," said Justice. "Going to have to pass."

"Dude, you can always siphon gas or just hotwire another vehicle," said Luke.

He shrugged. "Yeah, I could, but it's a pain in the ass."

"So, what, you're just going to hang out in this town?" asked Allie.

"No. Actually, I'm heading to Atlanta," he said. "See if they've found a cure yet."

"Don't waste your time," said Luke. "We were just there."

Justice frowned. "They haven't figured this shit out yet?"

"Not yet. The CDC has shut down and relocated," said Allie. "My sister said that most of the scientists are zombies now, and the few that are working on a cure aren't having much luck."

"Dammit," replied Justice, rubbing a hand over his face. "What the hell are we supposed to do now?"

"Hey, I'm sure they'll find a cure eventually," said Luke. "They just need more time."

Justice stood up and began to pace. "Well, I don't have time," he said.

"What, you have an appointment somewhere?" joked Luke. "Seems like all we have is time these days."

"No. I don't have *any* time to wait. Shit!" he growled, kicking one of the lower cupboards with his boot.

"Simmer down, man," said Luke.

"What do you mean? You don't have time for what?" asked Allie.

He stared at the counter angrily, tapping his fingers and then sighed. "I don't have time because," he raised his black T-shirt, exposing his lower stomach, and what appeared to be human teeth marks, "one of those bitches got a little too close to me in the last town."

"Oh, my God, you were bitten by a zombie?" gasped Kyle, taking a step back.

Justice dropped his shirt back down. "It certainly isn't a hickey," he answered with a cold smile.

"Seriously, though, it's not *that* bad," said Luke, amazed to have seen the individual teeth marks embedded on his bruised skin. "Did the zombie even draw blood?"

"Yeah, just a little. Enough to taint my blood, I'm sure."

"So, when did it happen?" asked Allie.

"Last night."

Allie bit her lower lip. "Do you feel any different – feverish or dizzy?"

He shrugged. "Had a temperature this morning. Luckily, I found some aspirin."

"If you're up and walking, you're doing pretty good, I'd say. My sister and I were both bitten and lived."

His eyes widened. "Really?"

"Seriously," she said. "We even went into comas and came out of it. Seems to me that if you're still running around and killing zombies, you're going to be just fine."

Justice sighed. "I hope you're right."

"See, you could join us now," smiled Allie. "If you really wanted to."

He rubbed his chin. "You say you're heading to Minnesota?"

"Yeah, then back to Atlanta to our new home, the Ritz Carlton. You join us and we'll make sure you get a suite with a view," said Luke.

"The Ritz, huh?"

Luke nodded. "Yeah. That's where the rest of our group is. We have a stockpile of food, weapons, and… the beds, *man* I miss those pillow-tops."

"Plus, we could always use extra help against the zombies and thieves trolling the streets," said

Allie. "I'm sure Tiny and Bryce would gladly let you in, especially if you help us get back there."

"Tiny?" asked Justice.

"Yeah," said Kylie. "He's a famous wrestler. Have you ever heard of him?"

He nodded. "Yeah, that big guy with the small voice?"

"Yep. He has a little bit of a lisp," said Kylie. "But don't mention it. *Ever*. He's a little sensitive."

Justice's lip twitched. "I wouldn't."

"So, you coming with?" asked Allie.

"What you're really asking is if I'll drive," said Justice.

Allie giggled. "Yeah, okay. Well?"

He paused for a few seconds and then nodded. "Okay, fine, I'll drive but it means that *I'm* in charge. When I say 'run', you *run* like the wind. When I say 'get down', you *get down* as quick as possible – no questions asked."

"No problem," said Kylie. "We'll do whatever you say."

"Yeah, dude," said Luke. "Just as long as you don't start foaming at the mouth or drooling when you look at us."

"Same goes to you," said Justice, walking toward the kitchen door. "Any drooling and I'm kicking your asses out of my truck."

"Too late," whispered Allie, staring at him with moon-eyes. "That guy is hot, Kylie. Don't know about you, but I'm already drooling."

Kylie just smiled. Even she had to admit, Justice was pretty cute.

3

"Well, it doesn't look like anyone's been back here," said Bryce, stepping over two zombies lying on Cassie's bloodstained driveway. It was hot and the stench from the fly-infested bodies lying around was enough to make him gag. It was nothing, however, compared to the restless angst knotted in the pit of his stomach. He'd driven like a madman trying to catch up to her, hoping that they'd somehow cross paths before reaching Minnesota. But the road back home had been pretty uneventful and there'd been no sign of anyone else still breathing.

Where was Cassie?

"What in the hell do we do now?" he thought out loud.

"I think we should go back inside and look for an address book or something," said Paige. "Maybe even a phone book, to see if we can find their grandparents' address."

"Yeah, but, do you even know their names?" asked Billie.

Paige shrugged. "The name *Wild* would be a good start. They live somewhere in Willow Springs."

Kristie looked toward the road and shook her head. "Dammit, where are those kids?"

The five of them, Bryce, Billie, Kristie, Tiny, and Paige had made it back to Minnesota in record time –

two days. Twice they'd had to switch vehicles, and a few times they'd had some harrowing encounters with zombies, but their determination to reach their friends and family had made them vigilant.

"What about your house?" asked Tiny. "Do you think they might have stopped there?"

Kristie shrugged. "I guess it's possible."

"Mom, they're probably not even in town yet," said Paige. "I'm actually surprised we made it back here so quickly."

Kristie's eyes filled with tears. "What if something happened to them? They're just children, and to be out there, somewhere, in this godforsaken zombie shit!" She turned to Tiny. "I don't know if I could handle it if Kylie was hurt. Or any of them for that matter."

He grabbed her hand and pulled her into his arms. "We'll find them, babe," he murmured, holding her against his chest. "All of them."

"Shit, looks like *we've* been found. Heads up, everyone – zombies approaching," said Bryce, raising his rifle.

More than a dozen of them were staggering in their direction from throughout the neighborhood.

Paige tightened her hold on the metal bat. "How do they do that?"

"They must smell us or something," said Bryce. "Let's get back inside and search the house before we attract more trouble than we can handle."

They quickly moved the SUV into the garage and then pulled the door down, but not before one of the zombies made it inside. The creature stared at the group as if he'd won the lottery and began to advance.

"Wow, did you see that?" asked Tiny as he shoved a large knife into the zombie's skull and twisted. "He actually had enough sense to duck underneath the garage door."

Paige scowled. "Just what we need – zombies with common sense. What *is* the world coming to?"

"As long as they don't start talking to us," said Kristie.

"Yeah, could you imagine? 'Give me your brains'," chuckled Tiny as he kicked the zombie's torso to the side.

"*You'll* never hear that from a zombie," smirked Paige.

Kristie scowled. "Paige…"

Paige's eyes widened innocently. "What?"

"It's okay," said Tiny. "Paige is just doing it to blow off steam. If harassing me makes life easier for her to handle right now, so be it. I'm not going to take it personally."

"It's *not* okay," said Kristie. "Paige, you need to treat Tiny with more respect. He's saved our lives at least a dozen times, and all I've heard from your mouth are smart-assed comments."

"Oh, lighten up, mom," mumbled Paige. "It's your fault, if anything. *You* raised me."

Kristie sighed. "I guess it *is* my fault. The apple doesn't fall too far from the tree."

"Nothing wrong with that," said Tiny. "I'd rather be surrounded with brave smart-asses than feel like I'm too intimidating to tease."

A loud banging on the outside of the garage door startled the group. As it grew louder and more intense, Paige covered her ears. "Now, who the hell is doing that?!" she hollered.

"Zombies," said Bryce. "They know we're in here."

"They're aggressiveness is obviously growing," said Billie, slamming the door of the Expedition.

"I didn't think they were *that* alert," said Kristie. "Usually they forget about us the moment we're out of sight."

"Maybe they're getting some of their human qualities back," said Tiny.

"Or just plain adapting," said Bryce. "I doubt they're actually becoming more human."

"Let's get inside," said Paige. "Those nosy bastards are really pissing me off."

They stepped into the house through the garage and then split up, searching for something that would give them a clue as to where the girls might have gone.

"Here," said Kristie, after looking through a box of old birthday cards in Cassie's bedroom. "This *has* to be them."

"Steve and Diana Wild?" asked Paige, her eyebrows furrowing. "I thought their grandmothers' names were Judy and Irene."

"They are. I think that Steve is Dave's brother. Steve Junior. Steve Senior is who we're looking for," said Kristie, shuffling through the cards. "Oh, here's one. It says 'Happy Birthday, Cassie, from Grandma Judy', but the address on the envelope is somewhere in Florida."

Paige nodded. "That's got to be her. Cassie mentioned she travels a lot. In fact, she was supposed to have been on some kind of European cruise when all of this stuff started going down. She didn't like talking about it, though. I guess her grandmother got the zombie vaccine before she left for the cruise."

Kristie cringed. "Oh. Well, maybe that was actually a blessing. Could you imagine being trapped on a cruise ship with thousands of zombies? There'd be nowhere to run."

"All those poor old people," said Paige. "How horrible."

"I don't know," said Kristie. "Henry certainly knows how to take care of himself."

"Yeah, but he's not your typical old man."

"True. Oh, here we go," said Kristie, pulling out a pink envelope. She stood up. "This has got to be the other grandparents. Steve and Irene – Willow Lake. That's only about twenty minutes from here. Let's go tell the boys."

As they turned to leave, there was a chorus of snarls and groans moving toward them from down the hallway.

"What the hell?" whispered Kristie. "How did they make it into the house? I thought all the doors were locked?"

Two zombies shuffled to the doorway as they sniffed at the air.

"Hhhhhaaaa….." gurgled one of the zombies, its foul lips turned up in pleasure as it found the source of the smell.

"Did that thing just say something?" said Paige, grabbing a metal lamp from the nightstand. She quickly unscrewed the finial, removed the shade, and then held the lamp in front of her. "Because I could have sworn it just said 'ha'!"

"I don't know. Dammit, where in the *hell* are those men? Tiny!!!"

"Hhhaa…." rasped one of the zombies, a bald guy about Paige's age with a goatee and black shiny plates in his earlobes.

"*Ha* yourself!" Paige growled at the zombie as it stumbled into the bedroom and reached for her. She raised the end of the lamp and slammed it down onto the zombie's skull, but it only stunned him for a few seconds.

"Hhhaa…"

"Oh, for the love of God," mumbled Paige.

"Hhhaa."

This time she rammed it into the zombie's left eye and grimaced as it fell backwards with the lamp still deeply imbedded.

"Paige!" screamed Kristie, holding up her lighter in defense as a second zombie moved toward it, staring in awe.

She stared at her incredulously. "Seriously, mom?"

The flame went out and Kristie flicked it again. "I'll bet this sucker used to smoke in his previous life," she said with a smirk. "Look at his face. Now he's having flashbacks, aren't you boy?"

"Enough, he's not a dog, mom."

The zombie, who was a tall, older guy with a pocked face and oozing sores, growled and reached for Kristie as she waved the lighter in front of his face a few more times. Unfortunately, he stumbled over the box of greeting cards they'd left on the carpet and fell forward, knocking both of them to the ground.

"Mom!" screamed Paige as Kristie pushed the zombie's chomping teeth away from her face.

"Oh man," shuddered Kristie, "you could really use a Tic-Tac."

Just then, Tiny charged into the room, reached down, picked up the zombie, and slammed the creature over his knee. The sound of bones cracking made them all wince.

"Oh, my God," said Kristie, as she stood up on shaky knees, her voice quivering. "I almost thought I was a goner there. Five more seconds in that guy's arms and he would have put a whole new meaning to 'sucking face'."

Tiny slammed his heel into the back of the zombie's head, sending what was left of his brains across the light beige shag carpet. "Sorry, babe," he said, wiping his boot. "There were more of them downstairs. They kept us pretty busy."

"Hello!" hollered Paige. "Can someone help me with this thing?"

A third zombie had slipped inside of the bedroom and had her trapped in a corner without anything to defend herself with.

"Hold on," said Tiny, grabbing a dark blue comforter from the bed. He threw it over the zombie's head, wrapped him inside, then picked him up and walked out of the bedroom.

"What are you going to do with him?" asked Kristie, following close behind.

"Babe, can you find something to kill it with?" he said, as the zombie struggled to get out of the comforter. "I think I may have twisted my ankle a little when I killed that last one."

As they reached the kitchen, Kristie reached inside one of the drawers and pulled out a large rolling pin. "Here."

Paige burst out laughing.

"No, that will work," said Tiny, setting the struggling zombie onto the floor.

"Don't ever underestimate your mother," said Kristie, handing the rolling pin to Tiny. "I've got me some mad skills when it comes to killing zombies."

"Amen, sister," said Tiny as he raised the rolling pin and smashed it down onto the zombie's skull.

"Everyone okay up here?" asked Bryce, holding a long metal crowbar covered in blood.

"We're fine," said Kristie, "What about you? You don't look so good."

He wiped the sweat from his forehead. "I'm fine. Damn zombies broke the glass patio door downstairs. Caught us all by surprise."

"Where's Billie?" asked Paige.

"Right here," he replied, stepping into the kitchen, looking just as frazzled.

"Did you guys block that patio door?" asked Kristie.

"Yeah, we moved the computer armoire in front of the entrance," said Billie, rubbing his bicep. "Sucker weighs a ton."

"Well, I found what we needed," said Kristie, holding up the envelope. "We should get moving."

"I'm going to leave a note," said Bryce as he started searching through drawers. "In case one of them shows up here, so they know where we're heading."

"Well, just tell them to stay put if they make it here," said Kristie. "We'll come back this way after checking Cassie's grandparents' and then my house."

Bryce nodded and began writing on a notepad when the loud banging began.

"Great, what's going on *now*?" asked Paige.

Billie walked to the window and looked outside. "Shit."

"What?" asked Kristie, joining him at the window. "Oh…"

Dozens of zombies surrounded the house, slapping at the wood and glass with their hands.

"They're going to eventually break through those windows," said Tiny, looking over Kristie's head. "We'd better get out before that happens."

The sound of shattering glass from somewhere down below confirmed their fears.

"Let's move," said Bryce, picking up the crowbar.

"Don't forget your bat this time," said Kristie, handing it to Paige. "It should be your new best friend."

She nodded. "Especially since my old best friend abandoned me."

Kristie sighed. "She didn't abandon you, honey. I'm sure she just wanted to keep you safe."

"Still," said Paige as they stepped back out to the garage. "She took Nora, why not me?"

"No," said Billie. "Nora took Cassie. It was her idea in the first place. She's looking for her father."

"I don't care whose idea it was," said Bryce as he opened the door to the Expedition. "They're both getting their asses chewed out when I find them."

"All of them are getting their asses chewed, starting with Luke," said Kristie, getting into the back of the vehicle. "Taking those girls across country when neither of them can drive, let alone shoot a damn gun."

"Mom, Kylie and Allie are definitely not victims. If anyone, you should feel bad for Luke.

He's already learned his lesson being stuck in a vehicle with those two, believe me."

Kristie smiled. "Yeah, when those two start talking, it can certainly make your head spin."

"Especially about boys," said Paige. "Both of them are so boy-crazy, it's ridiculous."

Kristie's face darkened. "Don't remind me, Paige. I don't need anything else added on to my current list of worries – two girls alone with a fifteen-year-old boy, hormones running wild."

Bryce put the key into the ignition as Billie and Tiny lifted the garage door.

"Get in!" shouted Paige as a group of zombies moved toward the men.

Billie raised his gun and began shooting while Tiny used his crowbar to defend himself.

"What the hell is that?" shouted Kristie, holding onto the dashboard as the truck began to shake.

"I… I don't know," said Bryce, staring down at the dashboard.

"Earthquake!" yelled Billie, jumping inside. "Pull out of the garage so we don't get trapped inside of here."

Paige's face turned white. "I didn't know Minnesota had earthquakes!"

Tiny jumped into the front seat next to Bryce. "Back out now, brother, quickly!"

Bryce threw it in reverse and the tires rolled over two zombies who'd lost their footing.

Paige threw her arms around her mother as the tremors grew more intense. "Oh, my God, are we going to die?"

"Honey, calm down. I won't let anything happen to you," she answered, closing her eyes.

Seconds later, the vibrations stopped.

"Well, that was odd," said Billie, staring out the window. Besides the zombies gathering around their vehicle, everything seemed so normal. As if the quake had never happened. "First zombies and now tremors in Minnesota?" he frowned. "These are some crazy days."

"Very," said Kristie, releasing Paige. "Hasn't been any of those in this state since the seventies."

"Is it going to happen again?" asked Paige, staring out the window at the row of grey clouds that were moving in.

"I don't know," sighed Kristie. "Let's just pray that Kylie and everyone else are safe."

51

"Dammit," said Bryce, rubbing a hand over his face. "This is getting more dangerous by the minute. What in the hell was she thinking of when she left Atlanta? When I get my hands on her..."

"Chill out, Bryce," said Paige. "It wasn't *just* Cassie who left, and besides, she was only trying to save the rest of her family. Don't try telling us that you wouldn't have done the same thing."

His face darkened. "I wouldn't have taken off in the middle of the night, and I certainly would have planned it out a lot better."

"*You're* the reason she took off in the middle of the night," said Paige. "She knew you'd try and stop her."

His eyes widened. "Oh, now it's my fault?"

"Well, you're kind of bossy," she said.

"Bossy? I'm sensible. Look, it's obvious that she *needs* guidance," said Bryce. "And the fact that she took off like that just proves it."

"Listen," interrupted Kristie. "Pointing fingers isn't going to solve anything. We've all done some crazy shit in the last few weeks and it was done out of desperation and the will to survive. Now we have to work together and find these kids before they end up dead or, God forbid, undead.

So quit with the dramatics and let's get rolling before you find out how frightening a woman out of cigarettes *and* on the verge of menopause can get. You all feelin' me?"

"Yes, mother, I feel you," said Paige.

"Me too," smirked Bryce.

"Good," said Kristie. "Now, let's see if we can turn our luck around and find everyone before it gets dark."

"We have about two hours," said Tiny.

She rubbed the sweat from her forehead. "Well then in two hours I want a drink in one hand, a smoke in the other, and everyone who's missing, accounted for."

"Right, I think that's asking for nothing short than a miracle," said Paige.

"Don't discount anything," said Kristie. "You ever hear about the power of attraction? Positive energy attracts positive things?"

"I've heard of it," said Paige. "Sounds like a crock of crap to me."

"Well, I don't know… they say it really works," said Kristie.

Paige snorted. "Well, if it really works, why didn't 'they' practice it a little better before all of these zombies made an appearance?"

"Maybe nobody was practicing anything positive when the zombie virus spread," said Tiny softly. "In fact, maybe everything that's happened is the cause of something much more intense than just a bad batch of flu vaccine."

"What are you trying to say? That this zombie apocalypse happened because of negative energy?" scoffed Paige.

Billie sighed. "I see where you're going – the world had already started going to pot before any of this, and maybe this is some kind of retribution we brought upon ourselves?"

"Maybe," replied Tiny.

"Well then who's punishing us?" asked Paige. "Aliens?"

"You ever heard of 'The End of Days'?" asked Billie.

Kristie sighed. "Yes, of course. But come on, zombies aren't a sign of the end of the world. I highly doubt they were mentioned in the Bible."

"What are you people talking about?" asked Paige. "Zombies, the Bible, the end of the world?"

"Nothing," said Kristie. "Don't worry about it."

"Just like I saw this special about it on the history channel – we will be struck by deadly plagues," said Billie, his tone grave, "and famines and earthquakes. The sky will turn dark and oceans will turn to blood. And finally, the Antichrist will emerge to fight the final battle between good and evil."

"That Antichrist?!" cried Paige, her voice shrill. "You mean, like Satan?"

"Paige," said Kristie. "Just settle down. It's not the end of the world, and nobody knows for sure that Satan is even real."

"Well, if he is, right now would be the perfect time for him to show up," said Billie.

"Oh, my God," moaned Paige. "The deadly plagues could be the flu that infected everyone, the famine could be happening now because fresh food is so scarce. And what about the tremors we felt earlier – what in the hell was that about?"

"Just chill out, you guys," said Kristie. "You're all making mountains out of molehills."

"And... the skies are definitely gray," said Paige, staring up into the clouds.

"It's summer in Minnesota," said Kristie. "Now, everyone, stop it! Unless the sky starts raining down scorpions, locusts, or frogs, I don't want to hear any more crap about the end of the world!"

Just then, a loud clap of thunder made them all jump and they watched in silence as the rain began to pour.

4

"Wow," said Nora, staring around in amazement.

The nuns had taken us to their church, an old cathedral on the other side of town. Candles lit the interior, and through the dim light, we were met with dozens of fearful but curious eyes.

"Lord above," said Henry, staring at the group of children who watched us warily. There had to be fifty of them, ranging from three to slightly younger than myself. "Where did all of these children come from?"

"Most of them are from the orphanage," said Sister Francine, the red-haired nun. "We brought them over as soon as we saw the signs. I knew they needed our protection through these difficult times."

The hair stood up on the back of my neck as her face took on a serene, almost angelic look. All three nuns believed without a doubt that the zombies were a significant part of the 'End of Days.' I, myself, didn't know what to think. It was certainly the end of something. Civilization as we'd known it.

"You really think that the world is coming to an end?" asked Nora, in disbelief. "God's wrath?"

Sister Francine nodded slowly. "Know this – in the last days, perilous times will come, for men will be lovers of themselves, lovers of money, boasters, proud, blasphemers, disobedient to parents, unthankful, unholy, unloving, unforgiving, slanderers, without self-control, brutal, despisers of good, traitors, headstrong, haughty, and lovers of pleasure rather than lovers of God. Does that not sound familiar?"

"Timothy," said Henry. "Paul's letter to Timothy. I know that verse well."

A chill went down my spine. I cleared my throat. "So, this is it? You really think this is the end for all of us?"

Sister Francine smiled and shook her head. "No, not the end, but a new beginning."

The door to the church swung open and two nuns rushed inside, looking upset.

"Two men are here," said one of the nuns. "Big men. They are demanding we let them in."

"Do they have guns?" asked Henry.

"I don't know," said the other nun, who appeared to be close to my age.

"Are there any zombies outside of the gate?" asked Nora.

"No," said the young nun. "Not yet, anyway."

"I'll go check this out," said Henry, raising his gun. "Let them know we're armed. You have to be careful of who you can trust, you know."

"Regardless, we will not turn anyone away," said Sister Francine.

Henry's eyes narrowed. "Are you willing to risk the lives of these innocent little children, Sister? There are some nasty characters running around. We've lost quite a few of our friends from murderers and vagabonds roaming outside of these gates."

"God has protected us this far," she said, smiling. "I have faith that he will keep us safe."

"Well, I stopped relying on faith the moment my parents were killed," I said, feeling my eyes mist up. "They were good people, too. They didn't deserve to die."

She smiled sadly. "God has a plan for everyone, child. It's hard to understand, but you must accept it and know that all will be revealed someday. It is his will."

"Yes," said Sister Theresa. "Each of us will be called to Heaven when it's our time. Some of us much earlier than others."

Henry's lips curled under as he removed the safety on his gun. He turned toward the door and started walking. "That may be so," he muttered. "But I tell you what – today is certainly not going to be *my* time, Sister."

"Wait, Henry," I said, hurrying to catch up to him. "I'll come with you."

"You just stay back and help protect everyone else, Wild," said Henry. "I can handle this."

"I really think I should back you up."

He stopped and turned to me. "Listen, if something happens to me, they're going to need you. Now, keep your gun close and don't let anyone in unless I give you the okay."

"Fine," I huffed. "But if you're not back in thirty seconds, I'm coming out there."

He shook his head. "Jesus Christ, quit being so goddamn stubborn, girl. You've done your share, now let the rest of us take our turns."

My eyebrows shot up. "Henry, you're in a church."

He looked up and nodded. "Well, the 'Big Guy' is going to have a chance to rip me a new one when I stand before him, which will probably be sometime soon, Wild. But for now, do what I say and you might save me from having to do a few more Hail Marys before we leave this place."

I nodded reluctantly, and then watched him walk out the door.

"Hey," said Nora, walking over to me. "If I were you, I'd forget what that stubborn old man said and go watch him. You know his vision is going and his reaction time sucks. I'll stay back here and keep an eye on things."

"That's what I was kind of thinking," I said. Plus, my stomach was in knots, the feeling of dread overwhelming.

I removed my gun from the holster and raced outside where Henry stood, talking to a couple of men through the thick metal gate. The tension in the air was heavy as I stopped beside him.

"Aren't you a sight for sore eyes, sweetheart," smiled a greasy-looking guy with long, dark hair, powerful-looking arms, and a teardrop tattoo under his left eye. "Haven't seen a real living woman in days."

"She's a young girl, not a woman," said Henry, spitting out a wad of chew. "Mind me, Wild, and go back into the church."

"No," said the other fellow, who was shorter, with red hair and an easy smile. "I think we should ask her the same thing we asked you, see if she agrees."

"No need to ask her," said Henry. "She doesn't make the decisions."

"Why is she packing then?" asked the dark-haired guy. "A girl who can't make decisions shouldn't be carrying a gun. What's the logic in that?"

"What's your question?" I asked. I loved Henry but I was eighteen now and didn't need anyone making decisions for me. Heck, not even Bryce for that matter.

Henry shot me a look of anger and I knew the words in his head were going to get him plenty of "Hail Marys."

"We need food and shelter," said the red-haired guy. "Haven't eaten in days and our truck is out of gas. We saw this church and figured anyone here would do right by us."

"Do you have any weapons?" I asked.

Red nodded down toward the bat he was holding. "Got me a bat, don't need anything more."

"What about your friend?" asked Henry.

The dark-haired guy reached behind his back and pulled out a revolver.

"Whoa, put that on the ground, nice and easy," warned Henry, raising his gun. "We don't want any trouble."

"Nor do we," he answered, removing the bullets. "Look, I'll let you keep this for me until we leave."

"Let them in," said Sister Francine, stepping around me. "The Lord wouldn't want us turning anyone away."

"Thank you, Sister," said the dark-haired man. "Much obliged."

Henry's lips curled under. "Fine, then. Toss your gun to the ground and kick it under the gate. No funny business."

"You all are a little paranoid," he said, kicking his gun toward Henry. "But I guess I can appreciate that. The world is upside down right now and trust needs to be earned. Don't worry, though. You have nothing to fear from us." Then he glanced at me and I shivered. Although he was smiling, it didn't quite reach his cold, dark eyes.

"You can probably keep your bat," said Henry, stepping away from the gate. "Case any zombies make it into the church grounds."

Sister Francine pulled out a set of keys and slid one of them into the gate. "Haven't had any zombies make it through, Henry. God's made sure of that."

"So has that heavy-duty steel lock," pointed Henry.

"It certainly helps," she said, with a small smile.

Henry grabbed my arm and pulled me aside as the nun opened the gate. "Listen," he whispered, staring warily at the men. "You and Nora keep a good distance from those two."

"Yeah, sure."

He raised his finger. "I mean it. See those tattoos under their eyes?"

I nodded.

"You get those teardrops in prison – when you've killed someone."

My heart skipped a beat. "Oh, crap."

"Oh crap is right. You stay close to Nora and the children. I'll keep my eyes on these two. As you can see, they both have trouble written all over their faces."

"Okay."

"What's your name, Sister?" asked the red-haired guy, as they stepped through the gate.

She smiled. "I'm Sister Francine. What are your names?"

"I'm Travis," said Red. "And that's Dwayne. Thank you for opening up your home to us, Sister

Francine. Looks like someone is looking out for us, answered our prayers."

"Their prayers? Pfft...rubbish," whispered Henry as we followed them into the church. "Don't like their slippery, smooth words."

"I guess we're not leaving yet," I whispered back. "Not while they're here."

He scratched his whiskers. "Got that right, kid. In fact, something tells me the nuns were right about God having a plan," he said. "And I believe that we may have just found out where he wants us right now."

5

"Kylie," said Allie, shaking her. "Wake up."

"What?" she asked, sitting up in the truck. Her eyes widened as she stared outside. "Oh, my God, Lincoln Park?"

Allie nodded. "Yeah, the guys left to go search for food inside of the zoo. We're supposed to wait in the truck."

"But, there's must be a ton of zombies swarming around this area," she said, looking out the window toward the zoo's entrance. "Why would they risk it?"

"Maybe not," said Allie. "There aren't that many cars in the parking lot. Obviously, many people were too sick to visit the zoo before they changed."

"Zombies, right there. See, I told you," whispered Kylie, pointing toward the edge of the parking lot.

"Well, they've been hovering over there for the past few minutes and, Kylie, they can't hear you," said Allie. "You don't have to whisper."

"Still, they give me the creeps. What if they notice us?"

"Just get ready to roll up the window if they start moving any closer."

It was hot, too hot to be sitting in a vehicle without air-conditioning, let alone with the windows rolled up. Because they were trying to save gasoline, Justice had forbidden them from using the air-conditioner. "The guys should be back here soon, anyway. They've already been gone for thirty minutes or so."

"I wonder if any of the animals survived?"

Allie's eyes softened. "If they did, they're probably dying of hunger. Those poor creatures."

Kylie stared at her in horror. "Oh, God, what if the zombies got to them?"

"Then they're probably either dead or zombies themselves."

Kylie bit her lower lip and looked back toward the entrance. "If they are zombies, let's hope they can't get out of their enclosures."

Allie stared down at her nails, which were bitten all the way down to the skin. "Because they're behind cages and glass walls, I'm sure the zombies never even got close to the animals."

At least, she hoped.

***

"Jackpot," smiled Luke.

They were in the zoo's cafeteria, which, although smelled almost as bad as the animal cages, still had a large supply of snacks and bottled drinks.

"I can't believe nobody has raided this place yet," said Justice, looking around apprehensively. There *was* a lot of food and some of it was in large plastic containers, as if it may have been recently packed for travel. He clutched his gun tighter.

Luke ripped open a bag of miniature chocolate chip cookies and groaned in pleasure after stuffing a handful into his mouth. "Oh, man, you've got to _"

The sound of gunfire caused both of them to hit the ground.

"Where'd that come from?" whispered Luke.

In a crouched position, Justice moved toward the entrance, which led to a giant atrium. "Outside somewhere, not exactly sure how close. We'd better get the hell out of here."

"But we can't leave all this food behind," he said, standing up and stuffing bags of Cheetos and popcorn down his shirt. "Who knows when we'll get this lucky again."

"I'd rather be hungry than dead," said Justice, looking nervously out into the atrium, expecting someone to come crashing into the building with guns raised.

"These days, you'll be both," said Luke, moving next to him holding three packages of brownies.

More gunfire from outside of the building startled them once again, and Justice swore under his breath.

"We have to get to the girls," said Luke.

"Yeah, I know. Follow me and stay close."

They crept outside of the building and bolted toward the next building over for cover, as more gunfire exploded somewhere close by. Seconds later, they both heard a loud, deep roar.

"Whoa, did you hear that?" asked Luke.

He nodded.

A lion or tiger.

Sadly, most of the animals they'd come across had either died of neglect or zombie attacks. Obviously, a large cat that was still alive after three or four weeks could only mean that it was loose and catching its own food, or someone else was feeding it.

"Let's get out of here," said Justice, wiping sweat from his forehead as he tried not gag. The stench from the rotting dead animals was enough to make him forget about any hunger pangs.

Nodding, Luke wrinkled his nose. "Seriously, I didn't think anything could smell this bad. Not even the zombies."

Surprisingly, there hadn't been many zombies at the zoo, and the few they'd encountered, Justice had swiftly taken out with the machete.

"Whoa," said Luke, a few seconds later as they rounded the cat area.

"That's messed up," said Justice, looking down into the lion's enclosure where several motionless zombies lay. It appeared that more than twenty undead had somehow thrown themselves into the lion's den to feed, but instead, had met their own demise.

"Why doesn't the lion finish off the bodies?" he asked, watching as a large male paced back and forth down below. "He must be starving."

Justice shrugged. "He must sense they're no longer warm, living creatures. Obviously he still killed them because he's a predator."

"I kind of feel bad for him," said Luke. "He's stuck down there, all alone."

"Well, he's been eating something to stay alive," he answered, pointing toward a large white sign. "It says there were three lions, total – two females and one male. Looks like there's only one lion in this den now."

Luke grimaced. "He ate the others?"

His lips thinned. "Looks that way. Survival of the fittest."

"He actually had to eat his mates," he said in disbelief. "I'd rather die than do something like that."

"He's a wild animal, but who really knows what hunger will drive anyone or anything to do," said Justice.

"I don't care how hungry I get," said Luke. "I'm not going after another person."

Justice opened his mouth to respond when he noticed a group of three on the other side of the enclosure. Recognizing the two girls, all the blood rushed to his head. "Oh shit," he said, pulling out his gun. "This is bad. Very bad."

Even from this distance, they could hear both Kylie and Allie sobbing as the man motioned toward the lion's den with his shotgun.

***

"No!" cried Kylie, as the older man commanded her to leap down into the lion's enclosure. "Are you freaken' crazy?"

"Jasper's hungry," said the man, raising his gun. "And I can't let him starve."

They'd been sitting in Justice's truck when the stranger appeared out of nowhere. With his neatly combed hair, kind brown eyes, and a zookeeper badge proclaiming him to be "Darren", they'd trusted him instantly and had gotten out of the truck. Then he pulled out a gun, and the next thing they knew, he was forcing them into the zoo because his lion needed nourishment.

"What's wrong with you?" sobbed Allie. "How can you do this? Are you on drugs or something?" The goofy grin on his face was definitely not normal; in fact, it made the hair stand up on the back of her neck.

The man shook his head. "Drugs? No, not anymore."

"Why… why are you doing this?" she asked again, relieved to see Justice creeping up slowly behind Darren.

"It's my job. To feed the lions," he said, smiling proudly. "Jasper needs to eat and I'm his caretaker."

"We're not lion food," said Kylie.

The sound of Justice's gun being cocked wiped the smiled off of Darren's insane face.

"Put the gun down," said Justice, holding the barrel of his revolver against the back of the man's head.

The man's lip began to tremble. "I... but Jasper... he needs to eat."

"He's going to have to skip this feeding," said Justice in an even tone. "Now, put the gun down, man, unless *you* want to be his next meal. I'm sure Jasper isn't that picky."

He dropped the gun.

Justice pushed him away from the gun and picked it up.

Kylie let out a ragged breath. "Thank God. I still can't believe you were going to feed us to that lion. You're almost as bad as those zombies."

Darren just stared blankly.

"Are you the only one here?" asked Justice, handing Luke the gun.

The man ignored him.

"What about those gunshots we heard?" asked Luke. "There must be someone else around."

"It was probably just him," said Allie. "He shot the gun up into the air a few times when we first refused to go with him."

"Hmm… Do you live here at the zoo, Darren?" asked Justice.

The man nodded. "Yes. I have to take care of Jasper."

"Yeah, we get that. Why don't you feed him something besides people?" asked Luke.

"There is nothing else," he answered, "and lions need meat to survive."

"What about the zombies?" asked Kylie. "Can't you just feed them to Jasper?"

"No… no… no…. Jasper doesn't like the dead people," he said. "Jasper likes the warm blood."

"That's sick," whispered Kylie, stepping farther away from him.

"Speaking of zombies," said Luke, "looks like we have company."

Two very gaunt and very naked zombies stumbled toward them, moaning and foaming green from their slackened mouths.

"I'll take care of these two, just keep an eye on him," said Justice.

Luke raised the gun and pointed it at Darren as Justice removed the machete from his belt and stalked off toward the zombies.

Allie looked away as Justice swung the machete twice with ease and the two heads tumbled to the ground.

"Hey!" yelled Luke as Darren took a few steps and then bolted away. "Crap, let's go get him!"

"No, just let him go," said Justice, wiping his knife on his jeans. "Don't waste any bullets on that weirdo."

"That's gross," said Kylie, looking at Justice's jeans. "Now you have zombie juice all over you."

Justice shrugged. "I need to change anyway. Got an extra pair in the truck."

Jasper began to roar again and they all turned toward the lion, who was pacing down below in the grass.

"The poor thing," said Kylie, peering over the edge of the wall, "he's all alone down there."

"It's so sad," said Allie, "and the only person he has left to care for him is a raving lunatic."

"I wonder if we can set him free somehow," said Kylie. "At least he'd have a better chance at surviving that way."

Justice snorted. "Set him free? Like that would work out."

"Yeah, maybe we *should* set him free, so he'll take out more zombies," said Allie, pointing toward the bodies below. "Look how he finished those off."

"You're kidding, right?" asked Justice. "Not only would he take out more zombies, but us and everyone else who crosses his path. He's not a tame animal –

he's a ferocious killing machine."

"We could find one of those lion whips," said Allie, ignoring him. "And maybe we could actually train him to kill zombies. That would be so cool!"

"I doubt they'd have whips here. That's what they use at carnivals, you know, for tricks," said Kylie. "Besides, that's cruel. I could never whip a lion."

Justice shut his eyes and rubbed the bridge of his nose. "Girls, we really have to –"

Allie grabbed her wrist. "Oh, my God, remember that time we saw Billy Jameson at the carnival with that tattooed chic and they were slobbering all over each other?"

Kylie laughed. "She had on those super-tight jeans and when she bent over, you could see the thong riding up her crack."

"That was so gross," said Allie. "Everything about her was sleazy."

Kylie smiled. "You're just saying that because you liked Billy."

Her eyes widened. "I did not like Billy!"

Jasper roared again from his prison.

"Aw… he sounds so sad," said Kylie, a sad look on her face. "And lonely."

"Lonely? Well, that's because he got rid of his two girlfriends," stated Luke.

Allie's eyebrows shot up. "What do you mean?"

"I guess they were jabbering away and just wouldn't shut up. Old Jasper must have decided he'd had enough," said Luke, with a sly grin. "So he ate them."

Kylie covered her mouth in horror. "That's horrible."

"Oh, I don't know," chuckled Justice as he began to walk away. "He ended up with food and silence. I don't know about you, Luke, but I'm almost envying old Jasper right now."

Kylie glared at Luke when he started laughing. "You actually think that's funny?"

"Little bit," he said, trying to wipe the smile from his face.

"So, um, did you guys find any food?" asked Allie as she hurried to catch up to Justice.

Justice pointed back to Luke.

"Oh yeah," said Luke, reaching into his shirt. He pulled out a sweaty brownie package and handed it to her. "Knock yourself out."

"Er... thanks," she said.

"Well, obviously we're going to need more than this," said Kylie as he handed her one, too.

"I've got some chips and popcorn, too. But, there's more in the cafeteria," said Luke. "I think we should go back and load up."

Justice shook his head. "No, I have a better idea – let's just get the hell out of here. Try our luck somewhere else."

"But we really need that food," said Luke, as his stomach rumbled, loudly. "My stomach is beginning to sound like Jasper."

"Jeez," said Allie. "Here, you can have the brownie back."

"Thanks. Justice, seriously, let's just grab one of those containers of food that was already packed and leave. We might not find anything else for a long time. The stuff in the cafeteria is ready to go and it would be foolish to leave here without anything."

"Fine," said Justice, changing course, "but keep your eye open for that wacko."

"Don't worry," he said, opening up one of the brownies, "my eyes are peeled for creepy guy."

The zoo was hot and eerily quiet, except for the constant buzzing of flies on dead carcasses as they made their way back to the cafeteria. Justice went in first with his gun raised and the other three followed close behind.

"It's clear," he said, lowering the revolver. "Grab what you can and then let's bolt."

"Oh, my God," said Allie. Squealing, she pulled out a candy bar and ripped it open. "You were just going to leave all of this stuff behind?"

Justice didn't say anything. He walked back to the door and stared outside.

Kids.

It was obvious to him that he was the only one who realized how dangerous their current situation actually was. Not only did they have zombies to worry about, but now they had that lunatic, Darren. From the way the guy acted, it was clear that whatever drugs he'd stopped taking, had unleashed some kind of madness.

Just like Jimmy.

His stepfather.

Jimmy had been diagnosed with schizophrenia only two years ago, but the family had lived with the psychosis for over fourteen. It wasn't until Jimmy's sister had been diagnosed with the same condition that their mother had finally reached out for help and gotten him the medication he'd needed. Before that, she'd always blamed his irrational behavior and outbursts on the 'Vietnam War.'

"I'm sure it's the flashbacks from the war, again," she'd say, after Jimmy had one of his episodes or nervous breakdowns, which were very sporadic. Sometimes he believed he was being watched by the government, and other times he wouldn't leave his bed for days. "We just need to be patient with him."

But it was hard to be patient with someone who took it upon himself to train children on how to survive the monsters lurking in the back of Jimmy's warped mind.

"You need to learn how to use a knife," he'd said when Justice turned eight.

Because Jimmy couldn't hold down a job, both Justice and his younger sister were left alone with him during the day while their mother had worked two jobs.

"No, please," he'd begged, horrified at the idea.

Jimmy had raised his finger. "Don't be a baby, Justice. Now, I'm going to throw this knife at you and you're going to catch it."

"Please, Jimmy, I can't! It's going to cut me!"

"Not if you catch it like I showed you. Now get ready."

"But why do I have to learn this?" he'd asked, scared shitless of the gleaming blade in Jimmy's hand.

"Because, that's what bad guys do!" he'd growled. "They throw knives at you and try to kill you. But you're going to be a survivor, boy. I'm going to teach you what my daddy never did, or your daddy for that matter. Now, pay attention and stop your sniveling."

And so they'd spent hours going over techniques that Jimmy promised would help him survive, should he ever get jumped by thugs or need to survive in a war. Oddly enough, all of the drills and combat training he'd forced upon him *had* helped Justice stay alive after the zombies showed up.

Unfortunately, Jimmy, who was one tough son-of-a-bitch, hadn't survived the effects of the vaccine. He'd turned into a zombie and Justice had been forced to kill him. It had been one of the hardest things he'd ever had to do, because deep down, he'd loved the man.

"You want a candy bar?" asked Allie, holding one out. "Chocolate makes everything a little better."

If only it were really so.

He smiled and shook his head.

Justice watched Allie and Kylie, and hoped he could keep all of them safe. They were still just a couple of naïve little girls, even through all of this mess. In a way, both of them reminded him of his younger stepsister, Amy, a little girl of eleven who'd wanted nothing more than to laugh and have fun. And she had, until Jimmy had turned into a zombie and had taken the lives of both his sister and mother. Jimmy had been the only one in the family to get the vaccine and the only one who'd died without fear. He could only imagine the complete horror his mother and sister must have felt when Jimmy had gone after them. Before Justice had gotten the chance to save either of them.

He blinked back tears and tried pushing the image of his mother's and sister's glossy blond hair and lifeless blue eyes out of his head, but it was difficult. He'd never forget finding them mutilated at the hands of Jimmy, who, ironically, had been the monster he'd taught Justice to defeat.

"Justice, you okay?" asked Luke, stuffing more food into a container that was already overloaded.

He wiped his eyes quickly. "Yeah, just got some dust in my eyes or something."

"We've got what we need," he said, picking up the container with both hands. His face turned noticeably redder from the straining weight. "I've got this one."

"I'll cover you, but we need to move fast," said Justice. "You sure you can carry that?"

"Yeah," he croaked. "Let's go."

"We've got some water," said Allie, struggling with a box filled with plastic bottles. "And I found a few diet sodas."

"Give me some of those," said Kylie, reaching inside. "You're going to drop that box."

"Thanks," she said. "It *was* a little too heavy."

"Are we about ready?" asked Justice.

"Yeah, why don't you make yourself useful and carry something?" asked Allie. "Like those paper towels."

Justice grabbed a roll that was sitting on the counter, and slid it down into his tank top. "Okay, let's go."

Thunder echoed in the distance as they moved to the door. Stepping outside, they noticed that the skies were now ominously dark.

"Looks like a storm is brewing," said Luke, glancing up as lightning flashed across the sky.

"Maybe we should hang out here until it passes," said Kylie. The clouds were moving quickly and the last place she wanted to be was in Justice's truck if there was a tornado.

"No," said Justice, feeling the hair stand up on the back of his neck. It was much too quiet outside, like an eerie calm before the storm. "This place isn't safe," he said, looking around. "I'd rather be on the road than stuck here. Besides, we need to get back to the truck, make sure Darren didn't screw with it. Let's keep moving."

"Oh, my God," said Kylie, turning to her friend as Justice began walking away. "Allie, do you still have the keys?"

Allie's face paled and she shook her head. "I… um… left them in the truck."

"In the ignition?" asked Justice, stopping dead in his tracks. He turned around. "Seriously?"

She bit the side of her lip and nodded. "Well… yeah."

He sighed.

Just then, Allie's face paled in horror as she stared past Luke, toward the women's restroom. Before Luke could turn his head, shots rang out and he dropped the container.

"Luke!" screamed Allie, dropping the box of bottles and scurrying toward him as he fell forward.

"Oh, my God," choked Kylie, covering her mouth.

They all stared at him in horror; it was obvious from the large bloody chest wound, that he was already gone.

"Oh," giggled Darren, who was standing behind a dumpster less than twenty feet away, a shotgun in his hands. "Guess he's staying."

Filled with rage, Justice raised his gun as he moved toward Darren and began firing, wiping the maniacal smile from his face forever.

"Luke," sobbed Allie, kneeling next to his lifeless form. She touched his cheek and moaned in grief. "Oh, my God, you can't leave us!"

Justice knelt down and examined the wound. "Yeah, he's gone," he said, his voice thick.

"Have you killed any of the monsters?" asked the child.

I'd been helping Sister Theresa feed the children peanut butter and crackers in the courtyard when the little girl asked me. She'd been sitting alone, clutching one of those American Girl Dolls like she was afraid it would disappear from her life, like everything else.

"Zombies?" I asked, not knowing exactly how to respond to that kind of question from such a young child. She reminded me of Allie when she was younger, with her light hair and dimples. Unfortunately, her hazel eyes were filled with a haunted sadness that made me want to cry.

She nodded.

"Yes, a few."

She clutched her doll tight against her chest. "Good."

"What's your name?" I asked.

"Kallie," she said, a shy smile spreading across her face.

"I'm Cassie," I said. "Do you have any brothers or sisters here with you?"

Her eyes welled up with tears. "No," she whispered.

She was obviously devastated and I was a complete moron for reminding her of what she'd probably lost.

How could I be so damn stupid?

Obviously she was alone.

"Oh," I said, sitting down next to her at the picnic table. I put my arm around her. "I'm so sorry, Kallie."

She wiped a tear from her cheek. "The zombies got my mommy."

"It hurts a lot to lose your mommy. I know because mine is gone, too," I said. "But you know what? I'd bet anything that they are both watching us right now in Heaven and smiling."

She looked up at me. "How do you know?"

"Because a little voice inside of me said that if I hugged you, we'd both feel better. I don't know about you, but I certainly feel much better now. In fact, I'm beginning to think that hug was actually from your mom."

She tilted her head, thinking about this and then her face brightened. "You're right. And that hug that I gave you was from your mom!"

"That's right. Oh, wait," I said, putting my arm around her and pulling her close. "I feel like giving you another hug. It must be your mom again."

She closed her eyes. "I miss you, mom," she whispered.

I smoothed her hair down and kissed the top of her head. "I'm sure that she misses you, too."

"Is that cute little girl yours?"

I stiffened.

Dwayne.

I ignored him and released Kallie. "Why don't you go and look for Nora? I think she's handing out water."

Kallie stood up and eyed Dwayne warily. "Okay."

"You look a little young to be a mother," he said as she scampered away.

"That's because I am too young to be a mother," I answered coolly.

His eyes swept over my body and I wished I had more clothes covering me. Because of the heat, my usual attire was a tank top and jean shorts. "What are you, twenty?"

"Eighteen," I said, raising my chin.

He smiled wickedly. "You're still legal."

"I'm legal but it doesn't make me available," I said, trying not to flinch as the pig's eyes traveled over my body a second time.

"She's also engaged," said Nora, who appeared beside me. "To a martial artist who could take you out with the tip of his finger if he really wanted to."

He looked amused more than anything. "A real tough guy, huh?"

I nodded. "Yes, but I don't need anyone's protection. I can take care of myself."

He put his foot on the bench and leaned against his knee. "I suppose you can, if you've survived this long. Truth is, I'm not a threat, so you can both just relax."

"Everyone's a threat," said Nora.

"Why do you say that?" he asked.

"Because we've both had our share of trouble in the last few weeks and they also tried giving us the same line of bullshit," said Nora.

His eyes narrowed. "Oh, is that right?"

"Yep," she smiled coldly. "Neither of us are naïve, defenseless, or stupid. So you can save yourself a lot of embarrassment and pain by taking what you need for food, and be on your way."

Dwayne reached into his pocket and took out a pack of cigarettes. "I think you have me all wrong."

"Maybe, but I don't really give a shit one way or the other. You've obviously been in prison and that tat near your eye, which you're proudly displaying, speaks volumes. So, if you think you're going to pull any wool over our eyes, you're wasting your time."

"I got that tattoo when I *defended* myself in prison."

"It's one thing to defend yourself; it's another thing to go bragging about killing someone using a tattoo, Dwayne," I said. "By the way, smoking isn't permitted in the courtyard."

He stared at me for a few seconds and then put the cigarette pack back into his pocket. "Can't believe I'm letting a couple of little girls like you bust my balls," he sighed.

"We haven't even started," muttered Nora as he turned and walked away.

"He gives me the creeps," I said.

She nodded. "Me, too. He's obviously dangerous. I just hope those *tards* leave soon, so we can get the heck out of here and back to Minnesota. I feel like we're wasting too much time here."

"I know," I said. Besides wanting to find my grandparents, my heart ached for Bryce along with the others. I just wanted to finish this mission and get back to the hotel. "But Henry is afraid those two men are a major threat to the nuns. We can't leave until they're gone."

"Well, they'd better be gone by tomorrow or I'm going to run their asses out of here myself," said Nora, her jaw set. "And I'm serious, Wild."

I wasn't sure *how* she'd do it, but there was no doubt in my mind that she would. "I understand."

That night we slept on the floor of the church with the children, taking shifts to watch over everyone. Since both men had been in prison, we didn't trust any of the kids alone with the strangers. Henry volunteered for the first shift, me for the second, and Nora for the final. When it was my turn, I wrapped a blanket around myself and hunkered down on a pew with the gun hidden underneath.

"Keep your eyes on those two," whispered Henry as we stared at the two sleeping men. "I trust them about as much as your lead foot."

I smiled and shook my head.

He smiled back and then his face became serious again. "Don't let them get you alone, Wild. I know you're good with those karate moves and everything, but those two are giants compared to you. It wouldn't be too hard for them to pin you down and hurt you."

I pushed the horrifying image away. "I'll be fine."

His lips thinned. "I'm serious. You didn't see the way that dark-haired fella's been eyeballing you. For all we know he could have went to prison for rape."

My stomach clenched. I hadn't even thought of that. "Well, one of them tries raping me, he won't live long enough to unzip his fly."

He chuckled. "I'm sure he won't. Just remember, though, keep your guard up."

"I hear you."

Henry walked to the back of the church, lay down on a pew with the pillow one of the nuns had given him, and within seconds was snoring so loud, I could hear him from where I was sitting.

Sighing, I stood up and stretched my legs, then walked over to where everyone was sleeping to check on things. It was early into the next morning and the children, all fifty-eight, appeared asleep. Two of the other nuns were also snuggling with some of the smaller kids as they slept.

"If you're tired," said Dwayne, who was sitting against one of the walls, watching me intently, "I can keep an eye on the kids for you."

"No thanks," I said.

His eyes narrowed. "You're just a young girl yourself. You shouldn't have this kind of responsibility."

"I don't mind."

"Well," he said, standing up. "I've got to go and relieve myself. I'll be back soon."

I nodded and watched him as he walked toward the exit. "Hey, there's a bathroom in the church."

"I'll go outside. I need a smoke anyway."

I watched as he stepped outside of the sanctuary, feeling uneasy. I didn't particularly like him wandering around where I couldn't see him.

"Cassie?"

I turned and found Kallie standing next to me, rubbing her eyes.

"Hi, honey. What do you need?"

"I have to go to the bathroom."

"Oh, well, okay," I said. I stood up and walked over to Nora, shaking her gently.

"My turn already?" she mumbled.

"No, I just have to take one of the kids to the bathroom. Can you keep an eye on the others while I do that?"

She said up and yawned. "Sure."

"Thanks."

Nora's eyes narrowed as she looked around. "Where's Dweeb?"

"Dwayne? He stepped outside for a smoke."

She sighed. "Great. Well, hurry back. Looks like I still have a couple of hours to sleep until it's my turn."

"Yeah, I know. Sorry."

"Hey, little girl needs to pee, she needs to pee," she said, smiling at Kallie.

"We'll be right back."

I grabbed a flashlight and took Kallie's hand in mine. We walked out of the sanctuary into the hallway leading to the bathrooms.

"Do you need any help?" I asked as we stopped outside of the small bathroom.

"No, but it's too dark to see anything," she said.

I handed her the flashlight, grateful that there were a couple of lit candles in the hallway so I wouldn't have to wait in complete darkness. "I'll wait out here."

"Okay."

She closed the door and I leaned against the opposite wall with my arms crossed, my mind wandering back to Bryce once again. I smiled as I imagined him tucking Bobby into bed, maybe reading him a story. Then I felt guilty for leaving my little sister the way that I did and sighed. She was definitely going to freak out on me when I made it back to Atlanta.

A loud crash from one of the rooms down the hallway made me jump. It sounded like glass shattering.

Crap.

Swallowing back a wave of fear, I tightened the grip on my gun and began walking down the long, cool hallway, which seemed more ominous with every step.

"Hello?" I called, raising the gun in front of me.

Nobody answered and I had to force myself to keep moving.

Maybe it was a cat?

I'd seen a couple of them prowling around the hallways earlier.

"Here, kitty!" I whispered loudly.

The sound of books or something heavy being dropped onto a hardwood floor stopped me cold.

"Sister Theresa?"

Silence.

With my heart hammering in my chest, I willed myself forward until I stood outside the room where I thought I'd heard the noise. It was dark, but from the shadows in the room, it appeared to be an office.

"Hello?" I whispered, trying to adjust my eyes to the darkness.

I heard the creak from the bathroom door opening back up and turned to see Kallie stepping back out into the hallway. "Cassie?" she called.

"I'm down here," I said, lowering the gun.

She aimed her flashlight at me and then let out a shrill scream.

Before I could turn around to see what had frightened her, someone grabbed me around the waist and clamped a hand tightly over my mouth.

7

The rain and hail pelted the SUV loudly as they drove to the other side of town, trying to locate Cassie's grandparents' home.

"Turn right at the next street," ordered Kristie, staring at the roadmap. "We should be passing a lake soon, and then they're only a few blocks from there."

"I can barely see the streets," said Tiny, turning up the windshield wipers. He leaned forward and squinted. "It's pretty bad and I don't want to hit any more zombies in this thing. Maybe we should pull over until the rain dies down?"

"Nah, we're almost there," said Kristie, biting the side of her nail. "So just keep driving."

"At least the rain is *normal*," said Paige, staring out the window. "Nothing to indicate that it's the 'End of the World.' Thanks, by the way, Tiny."

"What do you mean?" he asked.

"Scaring the heck out of everyone by talking about the 'End of the World.' I'm not ready for that. I mean, seriously, I haven't made it to college yet, partied until I've puked my guts out, or even made it past third base with a guy. I'm only eighteen and have too much living to do before actually dying."

"Seriously," said Bryce. "That's your 'Bucket List'?"

Paige raised her eyebrows. "What's a Bucket List?"

"The list of things you want to accomplish before you kick the bucket and die," he said.

"Obviously you've already marked at least one of those off of yours, Romeo," smirked Paige. "But maybe *I'd* like to sleep next to a toilet one night, making promises I won't keep or… reject scary, drunk-assed men who hit on me at a bar. Hell, even to feel the euphoria of getting a single line on a pregnancy strip before I find the real Mr. Right. There are just too many things I want to do in life before I die."

Kristie closed her eyes and rubbed the area between her eyebrows. "Thank you, Lord, for making my children so dramatic, cynical, and stubborn. If mom was here, I'm sure she'd say 'paybacks are a bitch, Kristie'."

Paige leaned forward and patted her on the shoulder. "Hey, you set the standards. I'm just trying to say that I want to enjoy at least the same things in life that you have before I leave this place."

"Okay, fine, I plead the fifth," said Kristie, with a humorless smile. "But seriously, honey, you should strive for better. You know, learn by your parents' mistakes."

"Yeah, but I'll bet you had a lot of fun making those mistakes," interrupted Tiny.

Kristie's jaw dropped and she punched his shoulder. "You are *not* helping. I'm supposed to be setting examples."

"Mom, it doesn't matter anyway. I'm an adult now and can make my own decisions – zombie apocalypse or not."

"Well," said Billie. "You've certainly earned your right after everything we've been through. Hell, we all have."

"You got that right, brother," said Tiny.

They drove for a while in silence, listening to the echoing thumps from the hail mixed with occasional cracks of thunder. When they reached the lake on the map, Tiny swore and slammed on the brakes.

"What?" gasped Kristie, gripping the dashboard.

Tiny pointed ahead toward the beach. "Tell me I'm wrong, but doesn't the water look pink?"

"Pink? No, that's ridiculous," said Kristie, trying to see through the wipers and drizzling rain.

Tiny put his foot on the gas and drove into the parking lot leading to Willow Lake's Public Beach. He then drove over the grass to the edge of the sandy beach.

"Well, yeah, it does look like an odd color," said Billie.

Tiny grabbed an empty glass from the cup-holder and opened the door. "I'm going to check it out," he said, jumping out into the rain. "Hold tight."

"Is this really necessary?" asked Kristie.

"I'll be back," he said, slamming the door. He then sprinted through the sand to the end of the beach and filled the glass with lake water. When he returned to the SUV, they all stared in horror at the contents of it.

"It *is* pink," said Paige in a strangled tone. "What does it mean?"

Tiny wiped the rain from his forehead. "I don't know."

"Relax, you guys. It could be a number of things," said Bryce. "Bacteria growing in the water, too much iron, dead fish, or even zombie contamination. Don't jump to conclusions."

Paige shook her head. "No, first the ground shaking because of an earthquake, now the water turning *red!* That's too much of a coincidence. This is it, we're all screwed."

"It's pink, not red, Paige," said Kristie.

"Your mother and Bryce are probably right," said Billie. "Let's keep trying to track the others and then we'll worry about pink water and quakes."

"Exactly," said Kristie.

"Okay," said Tiny, restarting the engine. "I know one thing for certain; we need to start searching the homes around here for bottled water. If the water *is* contaminated, we don't want to get near it."

"Whoa, check that out," said Kristie, pointing ahead.

Two rain-drenched zombies staggered toward the lake and everyone watched in fascination as they entered it.

"Weird," said Paige.

"Check it out, it's going to be over their heads soon," smirked Bryce, as the zombies stepped deeper. "Wonder if they'll float or sink?"

"Oh, my God!" gasped Kristie. "What in the hell are those idiots doing?"

Paige chuckled. "Fishing? Maybe they've figured out another way to eat."

"Maybe they're drawn to the water because of something else," murmured Billie.

"What do you mean?" asked Kristie, turning to look back at him. "I thought zombies were drawn to living flesh. You know, brains and all that."

"And blood," he said, smiling humorlessly. "Obviously, they're drawn to blood."

Kristie's face turned white.

8

They drove through two hours of hard and steady rain in silence until they passed a sign welcoming them to Rockford, Illinois.

"Just in time. We need gas," said Justice, breaking the somber mood in the truck.

"And I have to go to the bathroom," sighed Allie, who sat in the middle.

"Me, too," said Kylie, staring out the passenger window.

"It's going to be dark soon," said Justice. "Let's see if we can find a full parking lot and a toilet."

"And no zombies," said Allie.

"Big city like this is gonna have plenty of those," said Justice. "This is won't be easy."

"So, um, how much longer until we get to Minnesota?" asked Allie, biting the side of her nail.

He shrugged. "I don't know, we're still quite a few hours away. Maybe six or seven?"

"I hope my sister is okay," said Allie.

"You know, she is going to *kill* you when she sees you," said Kylie.

"I'm the one who should be mad," she answered, her jaw set. "She left without even telling me, and now that our parents are gone, we need to stick together."

"Did you lose them to the zombies?" asked Justice.

"No. A really bad man killed them. Shot them when they were trying to save my sister."

"There are a lot of dangerous characters out there," said Justice. "Look at what happened to Luke."

"You know… it's all my fault," said Allie, her eyes misting up. "I shouldn't have asked him to come with us. Now he's dead and it's my fault."

"Obviously it was his choice to tag along," said Justice. "And *don't* go blaming yourself for the acts of a psychopath. The guy was obviously messed up."

"I still feel horrible," said Allie. "And what am I going to tell Bryce when he finds out? They were so close."

"Forget about Bryce, Belinda is going to be the one who will be really upset. That's her nephew."

Allie shook her head. "No, it's not. Bryce just told her that so Belinda wouldn't shoot him. That's what Cassie told me."

"Okay, you girls are confusing the hell out of me," said Justice. "How many people have you had trying to shoot at you?"

"Too many to count," said Allie. She then told him their story, from the very beginning, starting with the first day of the zombie outbreak.

"And I thought the undead were dangerous," said Justice. "You guys have been through a lot of shit, especially your sister. I guess if she can handle being kidnapped a few times, getting bitten by a zombie, and watching her parents murdered, she's probably doing all right at the moment. Sounds like a tough chic."

"I hope she's doing all right," said Allie.

"So, what's *your* story?" asked Kylie.

He shrugged. "It's pretty boring compared to yours."

"I doubt it," she answered. "You can tell us if you want. Did you lose a lot of friends and family?"

He rubbed a hand over his face and sighed. "Well, I've always been kind of a loner, so I didn't lose many friends, just acquaintances and, well, my family."

"What about a girlfriend?" asked Allie, her cheeks growing warm.

He smiled grimly. "I lost my girlfriend long before the zombies showed up."

"What do you mean?" she asked.

He paused for a few seconds and then answered. "Well, she left for college last fall and decided she didn't want a long-distance relationship. End of story."

"Aw... were you heartbroken?" asked Allie, putting a hand over her chest.

His jaw tightened. "Heartbroken? No. She was too pushy. Always trying to change me and everything."

Allie raised her eyebrows. "Like… how?"

He shrugged. "Guess she wasn't crazy about the way I presented myself to other people or the fact that I wasn't interested in college. She probably thought I was white trash, since she grew up on the other side of the tracks. Her parents certainly thought the worst of me."

Kylie gasped. "Oh, my God, did they actually tell you that?"

"They didn't have to. I could see it in their eyes and the way they spoke to me. I'm sure they were relieved when Lexus went to college and I stayed in Georgia."

"Lexus?" snorted Allie.

He smiled.

"Do you know if she's still alive?" asked Kylie.

"Nope."

"I had a boyfriend before the zombies," said Kylie.

Allie's jaw dropped. "What?! *Who?*"

"Well, he wasn't my boyfriend, *yet*, but I know he liked me. He slipped me a note in class one day, asking if I had picked out a date for the Sadie Hawkins Dance."

"But the Sadie Hawkins Dance isn't until the eighth grade," said Allie. "That's like, next year."

"That's how I know he liked me," smiled Kylie. "He was already reserving a spot."

"Who was it?" asked Allie.

"Jason Peterson," said Kylie.

Justice's mind drifted away as the girls droned on about boys and dances they'd never get to enjoy. Although he'd been bitter about Lexus for months after their breakup, at least his high school years had been interesting. Unfortunately, the two girls beside him wouldn't ever get to go to dances, parties, or school sporting events. Everything in the world had changed, nothing would ever be the same for them and he suddenly felt very fortunate.

"Oh crap," said Allie, pointing ahead, as they reached downtown Rockford. "Looks like we've found where all of the zombies have congregated."

"Roll up your window the rest of the way," ordered Justice.

The streets and sidewalks were crowded with zombies in every shape, form, and decomposition.

Hundreds staggered through the rain, searching for food.

"You'd think the water would clean them up a bit," said Kylie, "make them appear less... gruesome. I don't know about you, but I think they look even more gross and disgusting wet. Especially the ones who are missing so much skin and body parts." She shuddered. "Yuck."

"They're pretty nasty," agreed Allie.

Justice tapped on the fuel gage. "If we don't find a way to fill up this tank soon, you're going to be getting a much closer view of these freaks."

Kylie paled. "What are we going to do?"

"Look for a parking ramp that's full and easily accessible," said Justice.

"Okay," said Allie.

Justice drove slowly through the downtown streets, trying to weave around the massive crowds of undead. When one of them walked directly into their path, he was forced to stop.

"Run him over," said Allie, as the horrible creature stared into the cab and began growling.

"You shouldn't do that," said Kylie, growing paler still. "It's still a person."

"No," said Justice. "What made them a real person has 'left the building'."

"But how do you really know that?" she asked. "Maybe they're still buried inside somewhere."

Allie's eyebrows shot up. "Oh, come on, Kylie! Look at that beast in front of us. He's walking with half of a skull and a missing arm. If he's buried inside of that thing, then he'll probably thank us if we put him out of his misery."

The zombie began climbing onto the front of the hood, foaming at the mouth as it stared at them with rapture.

"Oh, my God!" squealed Allie as the zombie crawled clumsily to the windshield and began licking the glass with its split tongue.

"What's wrong with his tongue?" cried Kylie.

"The forking? It's called bifurcation. It's a surgical procedure that splits the tongue," said Justice. "He obviously had it done before becoming a zombie."

Allie grimaced. "Seriously, he had that done on purpose? So he could look like a lizard?"

Justice laughed. "Yep."

More zombies took notice of them and began surrounding the truck, scratching at the windows and growling loudly.

"Oh, that is so totally gross," shuddered Kylie as another zombie stopped next to her window, his left eyeball barely hanging by thin, gray tendrils of flesh. The zombie opened its mouth and planted its wormy lips against the glass, as if kissing it passionately.

"Okay, that's it!" hollered Allie. "Justice, please take us out of here."

"Are you sure?" he said, glancing at Kylie, who looked like she was ready to hurl.

Allie nodded, vehemently. "Just get us out of here, *now*."

He stepped on the gas, tossing the zombie from the hood and hitting several others along the way. Unfortunately, as they moved into the next block, the "fuel" light popped on.

"Shit!" he groaned. "You've got to be kidding me."

"What…. what does that mean?" asked Allie.

He turned to her. "It means that we're screwed unless we find fuel. Right now."

"There's a 'Park' sign over there," said Kylie, pointing to the next street. "It looks like a ramp. We just have to make it to that building."

"Okay, yeah… we'll make that," said Justice. "Good eye, kid."

As they entered the next street, however, more zombies stepped into their path, slowing their progress even further. When they finally reached the parking ramp, Justice swore again.

"What?" asked Kylie. "We made it."

"The steering wheel is starting locking up," said Justice. "Yeah, we made it, but there's no way we're going any further."

They coasted into the entrance and stopped right as they reached the parking-ticket dispenser.

"The gate is blocking our path," moaned Allie. "And obviously there's no power to lift it."

"I *was* going to try crashing through it," said Justice. "But we've just used the last of the fuel. Looks like we're abandoning this thing."

"How are we going to do that?!" yelled Kylie as zombies began rushing the truck from behind, climbing into the bed and surrounding them on all sides.

Justice's head was spinning as he noticed an old, bald zombie who reminded him of Gollum from Lord of the Rings, especially when he opened his mouth and exposed several rotted teeth. As the zombie put his face against the glass and stared at him with longing, he felt the hair stand up on the back of his neck.

Precious...

"We have to get the hell out of here before more of these things show up," he said, turning away from the transfixed zombie. "I'm going to distract them and then you two are going to run."

"Run? Where?" asked Allie.

"Get to the very top of the ramp," he said. "The roof. I'll meet you both there."

"Why don't we try the elevators first? There's usually a door separating the elevators and the garage."

"You forget. There's probably no electricity for the elevators. We'll just get trapped inside with zombies surrounding us. Just meet me at the top of the ramp and we'll try to locate another vehicle."

"What if they get you?" cried Kylie, her lips trembling.

"I won't let them."

"But…"

"Kylie, I'll be fine," he said, grabbing her hand. "Don't worry about me. Just get to the top of the ramp and hide until I meet you both there."

She nodded reluctantly. "Okay."

He reached under the seat and pulled out Luke's bat. "Take this with, just in case. And here," he said, opening up the glove compartment. He pulled out a large hunting knife with a black handle. "I almost forgot about this."

"I can't use that," said Kylie as he handed the knife to her.

"You will if you need to, unless you want to die," said Justice, handing the bat to Allie. "Now, get ready to run as soon as the zombies start chasing me."

"What are you going to use to defend yourself?" asked Kylie.

"My gun and I still have the machete," he said, pointing toward the bed of the truck which was now completely filled with zombies. "I just have to get to it."

"How are you going to get out of the truck?" asked Allie, staring at the group of zombies pawing at the windows. "There's, like, over twenty of those freaks out there."

He pulled out his revolver and unlocked the door. "Like this," he said, slamming the door into the Gollum-zombie, knocking him backwards. "The roof!" he yelled, clamoring out of the trunk and slamming the door.

The girls watched as Justice shot Gollum-zombie and then two more.

"Look out!" shrieked Allie, as more zombies advanced toward him as he reached for the machete.

"I can't watch," gasped Kylie, covering her eyes.

Raising the machete, Justice began swinging and moving away from the vehicle while the zombies followed.

"Okay," said Allie, when the zombies had moved far enough away. "We should go, before they come back."

Sighing, Kylie unlocked the passenger side door and they both slipped out of the truck on that side.

"Oh, my God," whispered Kylie, as they crouched down. "More of them."

Three zombies had entered the parking lot with their noses in the air, sniffing. It didn't take them long before they noticed the commotion on the other side of the parking lot, where Justice was still swinging away. They stumbled in that direction, leaving the girls alone once more.

"Come on," said Allie, grabbing Kylie's hand.

The girls ran toward the next level of the ramp and ducked behind a van, when they noticed another zombie wandering down from the second level.

"Keep going, keep going," pleaded Allie as he shuffled closer to the van. When it stopped and began sniffing the air, both girls looked at each other in horror.

"Oh no, he must smell us," whispered Kylie.

A loud growl of excitement confirmed their suspicions, and seconds later, the girls found themselves facing a hungry and very scary giant of a zombie.

"Back off," said Allie, raising the bat. "Shoo!"

The lips on the dark-skinned zombie, who stood close to seven feet, turned up in a gruesome smile. He lurched toward the girls.

"Oh, my God!" screamed Kylie.

Allie swung the bat as hard as she could and hit the zombie in the waist. The zombie swayed slightly backwards but then steadied itself, growling angrily.

"Allie, try it again!" yelled Kylie.

This time she raised the bat over her head and hit the zombie in the chest, knocking him to the ground. "Let's go!" she cried, lowering the bat.

The girls ran past the zombie and continued their way to the next level, pausing only to gauge the safety of their path. When it looked clear, they ran to the next two levels until Allie stopped, gasping for air.

"I'm tired," she said, trying to catch her breath. "Let's walk the rest of the way."

"I hope nobody shows up and takes our food and water from the truck," said Kylie, wiping the sweat from her forehead. "I'm dying of thirst."

"Me too. I'm sure Justice will drive us back to the truck once we find another vehicle with gas."

"If he makes it," said Kylie, her eyes big.

"Don't say that. He will."

"Did you see the zombies entering the lot when we left? There were so many…"

"Justice will make it. He promised."

"I hope you're right."

They walked the rest of the way in silence, reaching the roof of the parking ramp. Both girls hesitated to step into the rain as they watched it come down in heavy sheets. The rain had obviously picked up.

"At least there aren't any zombies waiting up here to greet us," said Allie.

"Maybe they just don't like the rain."

"Maybe."

A growl from behind startled the girls. When they turned around, they found two gruesome half-naked zombies heading in their direction.

"Great," said Allie, gripping the bat tighter. "At least these two are a little smaller than that last sucker. He must have been a good basketball player being as tall as he was."

These two zombies both appeared to be women, one much older than the other, but from the neck down they were both so chewed up and rotted, they barely resembled humans, let alone females.

"I can't do it," said Kylie, her hand shaking as she pointed the knife at the zombies. "I just can't."

"Fine, let's just run," said Allie, grabbing her by the hand and pulling her into the storm. The girls' feet splashed through the rain puddles until they reached the door to the stairwell. When they glanced back, they noticed the two zombies hadn't given up on them that easily.

"Let's hide in here!" yelled Allie, grasping the door handle. Unfortunately, it was locked. "No... no... no..." she cried. "This is *not* happening."

"What's wrong? Open the door!"

"I can't. It's locked!"

"Oh no!"

Allie stared at her friend, whose wet, dark hair was plastered against her face. "We're going to have to kill them before they get us."

Kylie's eyes widened in horror. "I –"

"You have to!"

"Oh no. Oh, my God!"

The younger zombie reached the girls first and Allie stepped forward, her bat held high. "Leave us alone!"

The zombie ignored her and lurched forward with arms open wide.

Allie swung the bat and bashed the zombie in the head, crushing its skull. Horrified and disgusted, she dropped the bat as the zombie dropped to the ground.

The second zombie arrived and went right for Kylie, who screeched in horror as she tried jabbing at its chest with her knife.

"In the head, remember!" yelled Allie, moving toward it as it tried reaching for her friend. She grabbed it by its stringy dark hair, ripping strands out of the zombie's decayed skull. "Oh, gross," she shuddered, releasing the hair.

The zombie howled and then turned toward her, its mouth open and teeth bared.

"Come on, do it!" gasped Allie, backing away in terror.

"You leave her alone!" cried Kylie.

The zombie turned back to her and she raised the knife, plunging it into its head. Shaking violently, she released the knife and the zombie fell backwards with it still embedded in its skull.

"Are you all right?" asked Allie, rushing to her.

"I think so," she said, weeping. "I can't believe I had to do that."

"It would have *killed* you," said Allie as the girls hugged each other in the rain. "You had no choice."

"You two okay?"

The girls turned to find Justice limping toward them. They rushed over and both threw their arms around him.

"Oh, my God!" sobbed Kylie. "We were so scared!"

"It's okay," he said, patting her softly on the back. "I'm here, now."

"Are you okay?" asked Allie as they released him.

He gave her a lopsided grin. "Well, I almost broke my neck falling over a raised slab of cement but other than that, I'm fine."

Allie smiled proudly. "We killed us some zombies."

"I see that. Good job."

"It was horrible," said Kylie. "I hope I never have to do it again."

He put a hand on her shoulder. "I agree, kid, it's horrible, but you do what you have to do to stay alive. Don't ever hesitate if one of those things comes after you, again. They won't change their mind about killing you, and neither should you."

She sighed and nodded.

"What now?" asked Allie.

Justice scanned the lot, which held only three vehicles. He pointed to an old Ford pickup. "I think I can hotwire that one. Hopefully it has enough gas to get us out of this town."

"What about that car with the sunroof?" asked Allie, pointing to a newer Buick Regal.

He shook his head. "I feel a little safer in the taller truck with the crowd of zombies down there trying to get to us. Plus, I know I can hotwire the Ford because it's older. I'm just not sure about the Regal."

"Okay," she answered.

They followed Justice to the truck and found that it was unlocked.

"That was lucky," said Kylie.

"Why *would* it be locked?" said Allie. "If someone was going to steal a vehicle, they probably wouldn't go for an old truck like this." It was at least twenty years old and reminded her of Cassie's old clunker.

"Easy as pie," said Justice a couple of minutes later when the engine roared to life.

"What's that noise?" muttered Kylie, as they backed up.

"It sounds like it needs a new muffler," he said, frowning. "This thing is going to draw a lot of attention."

"Great, the zombies are going to hear us coming from the next town," said Allie.

"We'll trade it in as soon as we can. Right now, we really don't have a choice," said Justice.

"At least the tank is half full," said Kylie.

He nodded. "It'll get us out of the city. There will be plenty of vehicles in the next fifty miles or so. Lots of homes with trucks." He looked into the rearview mirror. "In fact, we'd better leave now. The noise from this beast has already drawn more zombies."

Four of them were heading in their direction, but Justice zigzagged around them, leaving the upper level of the ramp.

"See," said Justice, when he was forced to hit a zombie on the next level down. "Hitting one of those things with a car wouldn't be as effective. An old truck like this is much more practical."

"Ew… now there's zombie blood on the hood," cringed Allie.

"The rain will wash it off when we get back outside," he said, turning another corner.

"What about our supplies?" asked Kylie, who was sitting in the middle. "Are we going back to the other truck for them?"

He sighed. "No. It's just not worth the risk, and my back hurts, so now I'm at a disadvantage. Besides, when I left that area of the ramp, there were more zombies entering the lot."

"Well, I'm so thirsty," said Kylie. "I'm going to get nauseous if we don't find something to drink soon."

"We'll find something," he said. "Just hold tight."

"Okay."

When they exited the building, there were still dozens of zombies stumbling through the rain-flooded streets.

"Is this what it's going to be like from now on?" sighed Allie, laying her head against the passenger window. "Just those things and us, trying to avoid them?"

"Eventually they'll die out if they can't eat," he said.

She turned to him. "How do you know? I mean aren't they already dead?"

"Good point."

"It's not going to be like this forever," said Kylie. "God has a plan."

Allie raised her eyebrows. "*God* has a plan? And how do you know?"

"You'd know if you'd watched the History Channel more often," she said.

"I love the History Channel," said Justice. "But I may have missed the program pertaining to zombies and God."

"Well, it didn't really specify *zombies*," said Kylie with a wry smile. "But it did mention deadly plagues, which obviously did help create the zombies."

Allie sighed. "I give up, what has God got to do with the zombies and the world changing?"

"It's the 'End of Days.' Just like one of the historians on the show talked about."

"So, what exactly did they say?" asked Allie.

"They said we'd be struck by disease, hunger, and earthquakes. The sky will turn dark like night, and the oceans will turn to blood, and Satan will emerge to fight in the final battle between good and evil."

Allie's jaw dropped. "Shut up. Seriously? That's what they said?"

Kylie nodded. "Yep."

"That's kind of blowing things way out of proportion, isn't it?" said Justice. "I mean, you shouldn't jump to that conclusion just because a vaccine caused some pretty horrifying side-effects."

"Yeah," said Allie. "Don't go there, Kylie. Unless we get slammed with more earthquakes and the water turns to blood, I don't want to hear any more about predictions that you've learned about on the History Channel. It's scary enough out there as it is."

"Exactly. Besides, if the so-called 'Devil' or 'Antichrist' was here on Earth, I'm sure we'd know by now," replied Justice.

"Not necessarily," said Kylie. "He may have been around for a number of years and we may not have known. Like a snake, waiting for the right moment to strike. Who knows, maybe he tampered with the vaccine that created the zombies."

Allie felt the hair stand up on the back of her neck. "Okay, you're really freaking me out. Let's just not talk about this anymore."

"Fine, but –"

Allie closed her eyes. "Seriously. Stop."

Kylie didn't say anything more. Not even when they passed by a pink-tinged lake where two entranced zombies appeared to be heading.

9

"Just keep your mouth shut and I won't hurt you," whispered Dwayne, covering my mouth with his calloused hand as he pulled me into the darkness.

Although I'd lost my gun during our scuffle, he had no idea what he'd started. Weapon or not, there was no way I'd go down without a struggle. In fact, I'd purposely allowed him take me outside and away from the church, as I figured kicking someone's ass in a holy place *had* to be sacrilegious.

I nodded, trying to appear scared and as unthreatening as possible. The truth was, after everything I'd been through, I figured I could handle this with my eyes closed.

He dragged me around the church, and that's when he made his first mistake.

He released me.

I turned to face him. "What do you want?"

"Just to talk," he said, but the look in his eyes said otherwise.

I snorted. "Oh, that's how you get a girl to talk? You must have been quite the catch back in your hometown."

"I was," he said, moving closer with a sly smile. "Gals lined up to be with me."

I smirked up at him. "Lined up, huh? You must be referring to the showers at that prison you were incarcerated at."

His face darkened and he grabbed me by the throat.

Crap.

"That's not funny. Don't joke about things like that," he spat, his eyes bulging. "You have no idea what a man has to do to survive in a place like that. What he has to give up. No clue."

My eyes were watering. I tried digging my fingernails into his hands, but unfortunately, I'd bitten them down to the skin. I then tried to position myself so I could 'knee' him between the legs, when he suddenly released *me* and took a step back.

I bent over to catch my breath. "Sorry," I rasped.

"That's better. Apology accepted."

"No," I said straightening up. "Sorry that I underestimated you."

Then, before he had a chance to respond, I spun my leg around and delivered a roundhouse kick to his chin, using as much force as I could. He fell backwards with a grunt and I smiled in satisfaction.

Mountain boots, never leave home without them.

"You bitch," he growled, scrambling back up.

"Is that what they called you in prison?" I taunted as he launched at me. I ducked his attack, then turned and kicked him in the back of the leg, sending him into a prickly Evergreen bush.

"What's going on out here?" hollered Henry, who stepped out of the darkness with his shotgun raised.

"He, um, started it," I said, smiling sheepishly.

Dwayne stood up slowly, a grimace on his face. "Just wanted to talk is all. Had no idea she was such a crazy broad."

"If you knew what was good for you," muttered Henry. "You wouldn't call Wild a broad, *and* you'd stay away from her."

I frowned. "Hey, I'm also not crazy."

Henry ignored me. "Looks like you've overstayed your welcome, Dwayne. Now, you need to get your friend and hightail it on out of here."

He scowled. "I don't think that's your decision. Besides, this is a church. A place of God. He doesn't turn *anyone* away."

"Once you turn *him* away," said Sister Theresa, stepping around the corner of the building. "There is only darkness."

"*And* an exit door with your name on it," said Henry.

I just couldn't resist. "That' shouldn't be too difficult for him to find. Dwayne is *no* stranger to the 'exit door'."

He shot me a scathing look and I was relieved that Henry was the one holding the shotgun.

136

"I'm not sure what's going on out here," said Sister Theresa, her face solemn. "But this is a sacred church and we don't condone any immoral behavior. Now, for the protection of the children and our other guests, I suggest you and your friend Travis *leave* without giving us any more trouble."

"You people are all nuts," said Dwayne, shaking his head. "I haven't done anything but receive a few lucky kicks from this crazy chick."

"They were deliberate, not *lucky*," I snapped, putting my hands on my hips. "And *you* were lucky that Henry saved your ass or I would have carved it."

"Right," snorted Dwayne.

"Here's the other one," hollered Nora, clutching an ax as she followed Travis, who clearly did not look happy. "Kallie told us what happened and so I woke this one up, too."

"What did you do?" snarled Travis, getting into Dwayne's face.

Dwayne's face paled. "Nothing."

"He was trying to have his way with young Wild, here," said Henry. "I'd say that was *something*."

137

"I told you to behave here," growled Travis, grabbing the larger man by the front of the shirt. "To keep your shit in check."

"Please. I wasn't going to do anything," replied Dwayne with real terror in his eyes.

Henry and I glanced at each other in surprise. Although Dwayne was much bigger than Travis, it was obvious as to who was in charge.

Travis's shoulders relaxed. He released Dwayne and then turned to me. "I'm sorry. If I would have known he was pulling that shit, I would have kept a better eye on him. We'll be on our way."

I didn't say anything. Although Travis appeared sincere, something in his eyes told me that he was much more dangerous than Dwayne.

"We'd appreciate that," said Henry.

Travis nodded and then smiled at me. "You're a brave girl," he said, his eyes so black, they were unsettling. "I'm sure your parents would have been proud of you. If they would have survived."

"Well, I'd hope so," I said, wondering how he knew they were both dead. Of course, with the current zombie apocalypse going down, it was an easy assumption.

He studied me intently. "Something tells me we're going to meet again."

For some reason, I knew deep down that he was right, and it made the hair stand up on the back of my neck. "Oh?"

"Yes. Definitely. Now, don't lose that courage," he said, turning away. "If you want to survive for a time in this war, I'm sure they're going to need all the help they can get."

I was confused. "War?"

He motioned toward Dwayne, who nodded and then glanced back at me one last time. "You do amuse me, child. You really do. You and your antics. Unfortunately, sides have been chosen and yours is," he wrinkled his nose. "nauseatingly obvious. So, without further ado, I'm going to leave all of you with a parting gift, or rather, a message… for *him*."

"For me?" asked Henry.

Travis smiled darkly. "Oh, Henry. It's not always about you. Although I do appreciate your vanity, yes I do. No, this message is for he who creates such false hopes amongst his children. The one who thinks he can still destroy my master. He has no clue, however. No clue as to the powers that Apollyon possesses."

"Apolly-who? What in the hell are you talking about, psychopath?" snapped Nora.

Instead of getting angry, he chuckled heartily. "Exactly. We are living in pure hell right now, aren't we? You'd better all get used to it, because it's only going to get worse."

Before any of us could respond, he raised his hand and a small ball of fire appeared above it.

"Lord God Almighty, help us," said Sister Theresa, clutching her cross. "And have mercy on this man's soul."

"His mercy isn't welcome, here," smirked Travis, his eyes now glowing the same color as the flames.

Her eyes widened and she held out her cross. "Be gone, demon!"

We all watched in stunned disbelief as he raised his other hand and began spinning the fire until it was the size of a large beach ball. Then he turned toward the church and cast it into the air.

"No!" I screamed, as the fireball hit the side of the church and the flames began to spread.

He looked back at us and his smile chilled me to the bone. "Well, good luck with all of that." Then he left, his laughter echoing wickedly in the darkness.

10

ALLIE AND KYLIE

After leaving the disturbing scene at the lake, they quickly found the street leading to Cassie and Allie's grandparents' home.

"There's the house," said Kristie, pointing to a small cedar home nestled halfway up the block.

"Looks pretty quiet around here," murmured Tiny. "I don't know if that's a good sign or a really bad one."

"Not a lot of zombies lurking around is definitely good for us," said Bryce, getting out of the SUV.

The rest of them got out of the vehicle and splashed through the deep puddles until they reached the front porch.

"Should we knock?" asked Tiny, cupping his hands around his eyes as he tried looking through a large bay window.

"Why not? It'll draw the attention of any zombies in the house and we'll know what we're dealing with," said Kristie, rapping on the door.

"Ring the doorbell, too, in case someone is in the back of the house," said Bryce.

After ringing and knocking several times, they walked around the back to the three-season porch. Fortunately, the backdoor wasn't locked.

"Let's just go inside," said Kristie, pushing the door open. When they entered the living room, she sighed. "Hate to say this, but something tells me we're all alone in here."

"Keep going," said Paige. "Maybe they're downstairs or in one of the other rooms."

"Maybe," her mother replied.

They walked toward the back of the house until they reached the kitchen.

"Check this out," said Bryce, picking up a piece of paper. "They left a note."

To our loved ones,

If you're reading this then our prayers have been answered, and you're alive! As you can see, we are not at the house but have taken refuge with Tom and Barb on their yacht (Her Escape) on the Saint Croix River. We have stockpiled some supplies and have anchored near the Stillwater Bridge, so if you can join us, please do, because we miss and love you so very much!
Hugs and Kisses,
Us

Bryce sighed. "Great. Well, I guess we have some more driving to do."

"Hmm... It's going to be dark soon and I think we should wait around here a little longer," said Kristie. "In case Kylie and Allie show up."

"Or, Bryce and I could drive to Stillwater right now and look for the yacht, while the rest of you hold tight here," said Billie.

Tiny shook his head. "I don't think it's a good idea to split up. What if something bad happens or if one of you get hurt? Then you guys would be missing, too."

"If we sit around here, we're wasting more time," said Bryce. "Billie and I should leave right now, in case Cassie and Nora have already headed out to Stillwater and need help. We wait too long, and we may miss them totally."

"Yeah, he's right," said Kristie. "Knowing Cassie, once she knows her grandparents are safe, she'll head back to Atlanta. You forget, she doesn't even know that her sister is missing, again."

"Maybe they've already reunited," said Tiny.

"No," replied Bryce. "I doubt those kids made it to Minnesota before we did."

"You've convinced me," said Tiny, throwing the keys to Bryce. "Leave us some food and water before you take off, though."

"Sure," said Bryce.

"I'm coming with you guys," said Paige.

"Absolutely *not*, young lady," said Kristie.

She rolled her eyes. "For God's sake, mom! I'm not sitting here, watching you two play kissy-face while these guys go off to find Cassie. Besides, like I said earlier, I'm an adult now and should have the right to make my own decisions."

"You're still my kid. Look, it's too dangerous out there. You're staying here with us and that's final," said Kristie.

Paige's face fell. "You never let me do anything. I mean, come on, haven't I proved that I can protect myself against the zombies?"

"Listen, it's not just the zombies I'm worried about, Paige. Look at what happened to you and Cassie in Atlanta. There are some dangerous people out there and I'm not taking any chances of you getting hurt. I mean, hell, we don't even know where your sister is! I'm not about to lose you out there, too. So just chill out here with us and stop trying to take on everything."

Paige stared at her for a minute and then nodded. "Fine."

Kristie walked over and pulled her into her arms. "Thank you. Now, why don't you help Tiny gather some food from the SUV before these two take off. Then, if I were you, I'd try and get some rest. I can't even remember the last time you slept."

"Well. I am kind of tired."

"I bet. While you guys do that, I'm going to see if there are any candles around," said Kristie, opening some drawers in the kitchen. "It's going to be dark soon and we'll be walking into walls if we don't have light."

Tiny handed her a flashlight. "Take this and check the laundry room, too," said Tiny. "That's where I usually kept my candles."

Paige followed the guys back out to the SUV where they grabbed a jug of water, some beef jerky, and a bag of popcorn.

"At least the rain stopped," said Bryce, staring up into the sky.

"For now," said Paige.

"So, we should be back in a couple of hours," said Billie, getting into passenger side of the SUV. "I would think all of that food would tide you guys over until then."

"I'd use the bathroom here if I were you two," said Paige, leaning into the window. "Stillwater is almost an hour away."

Billie sighed and then got back out of the SUV. "Probably a good idea."

"She's right," said Bryce. He smiled. "For once."

"You're a barrel of laughs, Mr. Miyagi," she said, with a smirk.

Bryce's eyes narrowed. "Didn't your mother tell you to go take a nap or something?"

"Yes she did, and for once, I'm not going to argue."

"Amazing," he said, getting back out of the SUV.

When they walked back into the house, Paige told Kristie that she was going to lie down in one of the bedrooms.

"Okay, honey. I'll wake you up if I hear anything."

She kissed her mom on the cheek. "Love you, mom."

Kristie smiled. "I love you, too, Paige."

Fifty minutes later, as Bryce maneuvered the SUV around a group of zombies in downtown Stillwater, Kristie brought a candle into the bedroom Paige had disappeared into, only to find it empty.

"Paige?" she hollered, checking the other rooms in the house. "Paige!"

"What's wrong?" asked Tiny, chewing on a piece of dried beef.

She rubbed her forehead in frustration. "I think that Paige took off with the boys."

"Oh shit."

She sat down on one of the recliners and sighed. "I should have known something was wrong when she gave up so easily earlier when I told her she couldn't go with them to Stillwater. She's usually not so compliant. I should have known she was up to something."

Tiny rubbed her back. "Don't worry about Paige, hon. I'm sure the boys will take good care of her."

She looked up at him. "They'd better, because when she gets back, I swear, I'm going to tear into her harder than any freaken' zombie, dammit."

***

"Is that the boat?" asked Billie, thirty minutes later.

They'd parked on the Stillwater Bridge overlooking the river and there was an older model fifty-seven foot Jefferson anchored in the water.

Bryce lowered the binoculars. "Yep, that's the one. *Her Escape.*"

"You see anyone?"

He shook his head. "No. It's too dark. They could all be sleeping. It's after ten."

"Let's hope that's all it is."

"You should park at the marina over there," said Paige, over Billie's shoulder.

"Jesus!" he gasped, turning around.

"Paige!" barked Bryce. "You scared the hell out of us. What are you doing here?"

She smiled. "I'm here to help. Chill out."

"Did you tell your mom you were coming?" asked Bryce.

She snorted. "Hell no."

"When did you sneak into the SUV?" asked Bryce.

"When you guys were relieving yourselves in the house."

"Figures."

"Kristie must be worried sick," said Billie. "You shouldn't have done this."

"Look, there was no way I was going to stay behind picking my butt while you guys took off to go where the action is. No way."

"Is that what girls do when they're bored?" laughed Billie. "Pick their butts?"

She pushed his shoulder. "Oh, shut up, you nerd."

"Paige, this is dangerous," said Bryce, motioning to a pack of zombies already moving toward them from across the bridge. "It's not an adventure or a game. It's real life and death situations. Now, not only do we have to worry about finding the others, but we have to worry about you."

Her eyes flashed angrily. "Why does everyone assume that I can't take care of myself?"

"I'm sure you can, to a point. But when you're surrounded by zombies and neither of us can get to you, what are you going to do? Swing the bat and hope for the best? I don't want to sound sexist, but you're a girl, and not even a very big one," said Bryce.

"I'm five-ten, so I'm not that small, and definitely not stupid. For God's sake, I'm not just going to put myself in a dangerous situation."

Bryce threw up his hands. "What do you think you're doing now?!"

"Calm down," said Billie. "What's done is done and we have to move forward. Let's find a place to park at that marina. Paige can wait in the

SUV while we walk to the river's edge and try to get their attention."

"I'm *not* waiting in the SUV," said Paige. "I'm coming with you guys."

"Oh, *hell* no," said Bryce.

"I have to agree with Bryce. That's where we draw the line."

Paige sighed. "Fine."

"We're serious, Paige. Stay in the vehicle," warned Bryce.

"Heard you the first time," she yawned.

"Good," he replied, turning on the engine. "Because I'm not going to save your ass if you disobey. Seriously. I don't care if Kristie kills me because of it. I have too many other people to worry about these days."

"I get it."

Knowing how unruly Paige's best friend was, Bryce wasn't so sure.

11

ALLIE AND KYLIE

"Shit," said Justice, tapping on the gas gauge, thirty minutes out of Rockford. "I think we're running out of gas already."

Allie leaned over and looked at the gauge. "Why does it say that it's half-full, then?"

"Must be broken."

"Are we going to make it to the next town?" asked Kylie, staring into darkness, which held nothing but fields, trees, and the walking dead.

"I don't think so," he said. "I think we're screwed."

"How far is it to the next town?" asked Allie.

"Janesville is another thirty miles, but we should be able to find an abandoned vehicle along the way. A farmstead or *something*," he replied.

"We have to walk?" squeaked Kylie, in horror. "In the darkness, all alone?"

He shrugged. "Well, you can wait in the truck until I come back with something more suitable."

"Oh no," she said. "Been there, done that. We're coming with you."

Within minutes, the truck began to coast on the fumes alone. When it finally stalled, they got out of the truck and started walking.

"Pace yourself," he said, staring forward into the darkness. "We probably have a very long walk a head of us."

"It's so dark," said Kylie, biting her lower lip. "And there are so… many trees. Anything could be lurking in there, waiting for the right time to attack us."

"True, so keep your eyes open," he replied, "and your voices down."

"At least it's not raining anymore," whispered Allie.

"Yeah, but it left us with the smell of dead fish," he said, wrinkling his nose. "Hell, the smells on this planet just keep getting better and better every day."

"And copper," said Kylie. "It smells like copper, too."

Justice sighed. "You're not going to start with that bloody water thing again, are you?"

"Why can't you open your mind along with your eyes?" she said. "This is only the beginning of what's going to happen. A beginning to an end."

"Dun, dun, dun..." chuckled Justice.

"You really think this is the end of the world?" whispered Allie, a knot forming in her stomach. She was exhausted and Kylie's fanatical predictions were starting to really get to her.

Kylie's eyes glittered in the darkness. "Well, I believe that it's the end of *something* and that the zombies are just the prequel. Soon, we're going to be in the middle of something so profound, something that is going to change the rest of humanity forever. For some, it's going to be exhilarating and beautiful, for others, it's going to be devastating."

Allie stopped in her tracks. "Okay, you're beginning to really freak me out. I've never heard you talk like that. You sound so… prophetic. Is that even a word?"

She smiled. "Yes."

"So, this is all of the stuff you watched on the History Channel?" asked Justice.

"Um, well… a little. But, I know you're both going to think I'm crazy…"

"What?" asked Allie.

"I've been having these dreams," she said. "Crazy wild dreams, about war and death."

"War and death?" frowned Allie. "Seriously? That sounds so morbid."

She nodded. "I know, right? I've had several these last couple of weeks. I've dreamt about, now don't laugh, but angels fighting demons. Demons that are being led by Satan."

Justice's eyebrows shot up. "Satan? Oh boy. Look, I'm going to be honest with you – I'm an atheist. A firm atheist. So obviously I'm going to tell you that your mind is playing tricks on you.

That there is no such thing as the Devil, demons, or even *God*."

"Seriously?" asked Allie, turning to him. "You really believe that?"

"Of course. If there was a God, why would he have allowed so many people to die? Innocent people. And don't tell me that only the really wicked ones were killed, because my little sister was as sweet and virtuous as they come," he said, his eyes moistening up. "She didn't deserve to die the way she did, with her throat and insides ripped out."

"I'm sorry," said Kylie, touching his arm. "You know that we've all lost people we loved. But you have to believe that it was part of a plan. One bigger than all of us."

"No," he said, his voice thick. "I'm sorry but I just won't buy into that. We're alone, *all* alone… and when we die, we die. Everything about us dies and those are the facts."

Kylie frowned. "But –"

"No more talk, please," he said, moving ahead of them. "Just, please, respect my beliefs by keeping yours to yourself."

Allie and Kylie stared at each other silently and then began walking again.

"I'm not saying that I don't believe you had those dreams," whispered Allie. "But you have to admit, all this talk about the end of the world and a fight between good and evil, it's just too much."

She nodded. "I know, but Allie, I swear to you, these dreams are so vivid, so real. I'm not psychic, but I believe that someone is sending me a real message. One that's very relevant to what's been happening."

"A message, from who?" asked Allie.

She looked up at the stars. "Someone up there, who's looking out for us."

12

"Is that the last of the kids?" asked Henry, bending over and trying to catch his breath.

I stared into the darkness at all of the children, many of them peering back at me with tear-stained faces. "Yes. Everyone's accounted for. Nora said in a few minutes, we should be able to bring everyone back inside. Are you okay?"

Fortunately, we'd gotten the flames out with hoses and wet blankets before the fire had caused any real damage to the church.

He stood up straight and wiped the sweat from his forehead with the back of his hand. "Oh, I'm fine. The real question is – what in the hell happened back there, Wild?"

I shook my head. "I don't really know, Henry. I've already pinched myself several times, to make sure I'm not dreaming. Right now, I almost wish I was."

"That feller, Travis? He must be some kind of magician or illusionist to pull something like that off."

"Something. He certainly was a whack-job."

"Both of them were," he said.

"At least they're gone now," I said.

He took his cowboy hat off, ran a hand through his white hair, then plopped it back in place. "Well, I don't know about you, but I'm exhausted. I think we should all try and get some sleep, then head on out of here before noon. Get back to Minnesota."

"I agree, but what if those guys come back and cause more trouble for the nuns?" I whispered.

"You know, something tells me that they're not coming back this way. No, I think they've got bigger fish to fry and this was just a little pit-stop."

"You really think so?"

He nodded.

"What about you, Nora?" I asked, as she walked over to us. "What'd you make of those two guys?"

Her eyes narrowed. "Tell you the truth, that dude, Travis, he seriously gave me the chills."

I raised my eyebrows. "He even freaked you out, huh?"

"Hell yeah. The way he handled the big dufus, and that ball of fire he somehow conjured up… that was some strange shit."

"Sister Theresa called him a demon," I said. "You don't think there was anything to that?"

Nora burst out laughing. "Seriously, Wild? A freaken' demon? What funny plants have you been smoking, girl?"

I frowned. "Well, if I would have mentioned zombies three months ago, you would have laughed at me then, too."

Her smile fell. "Good point."

Henry waved his hand in disgust. "Okay, enough demon-mumbo-jumbo talk. That guy was some kind of illusionist, just like I told Wild. That's all it is. Why do you think he had that tattoo under his eye? Been in prison, obviously. If he was a demon, you think he would have ended up in the slammer? Hell no."

"Maybe you're right," I said. "I'm just being paranoid. That stuff the nuns were talking about earlier, it's been niggling at me all night."

"Listen, Wild, those two yahoos were just trying to scare the tar out of us. Obviously, they did a good job. Even left me a little miffed. But now we know better, right? It's just illusion brought on by an evil man. One that is certainly human, but nothing more."

I nodded.

"Okay," he said. "Now, I'm tuckered. I'm going to lie down for an hour or two. When I'm refreshed, we're going to make sure these women have what they need to keep those kids safe for a while. Then, we're going to get back to our original mission – find your grandparents, Nora's old man, and then get our butts back to Atlanta."

Thinking of how much I missed my sister and Bryce, I couldn't agree more.

He stared off into the darkness, a wistful look on his face. "I tell you what – I sure miss watching Belinda do those Pilates moves, by golly. I don't even have to exercise – she squats and it's all that's needed to get this old man's blood flowing."

I bit back a smile as Henry started shuffling toward the church.

13

"Do you think she'll stay put?" asked Billie as they skidded down the mud-covered hill and through the trees.

Fortunately, the boat was anchored in a spot that was accessible, although not easily on foot. Thus, their trek had been more challenging than they'd originally anticipated.

"She'd better or she's going to have more than the zombies to worry about. If she doesn't fall going down this hill, then she'll fall backwards when I rip into her about defying us."

Billie chuckled. "Somehow, I don't think you scare her."

"I must be losing my touch," said Bryce with a humorless grin. "I can't keep any of these girls in line."

"They're all pretty unruly. I'm surprised they've made it this far, being so reckless."

"If you ask me, they've just been really lucky."

"Well, I don't know about just being lucky. Nora, Cassie, and Paige are pretty tough chicks. They put a lot of men I've met to shame."

"Yeah, well they're also overly-confident when it comes to these zombies. I mean, seriously, one false move and that's it. Tar-tar for the zombies. They all need to start thinking before acting."

"I hear you."

When the guys reached the bottom of the hill, they moved to the edge of the water and Bryce took out his flashlight.

"The water," whispered Billie. "It's pink again, isn't it?"

Bryce shined it at the water near their feet and nodded. "Yeah, it kind of looks that way."

Billie frowned. "I can't believe this. What in the heck is going on?"

"Just relax, man. Don't go jumping to conclusions."

"It's hard not to after everything that has happened."

He shook the flashlight several times to charge it. "We have to focus on finding the girls right now. We'll worry about this other stuff later."

Billie's eyes widened and he pointed. "Oh, my God, what in the hell is that?"

Bryce aimed the flashlight toward the moonlit water and felt the hair stand up on the back of his neck. "I, um, believe those are a couple of zombies enjoying a midnight swim."

"That's pretty creepy," he said, watching the zombies, who were wading out into deeper water.

"Yeah, a little bit."

"Wonder if zombies got to the people on the boat?"

"I guess we'll soon find out. "Hello!" he called, aiming the flashlight toward the dark yacht.

Nobody answered.

"Hello!" he yelled louder, his voice echoing across the water.

"This doesn't look good," muttered Billie after a few minutes of silence.

"No, it doesn't," he said, handing him the flashlight. "Here, hold this."

"What are you going to do?"

Bryce lifted his gray T-shirt over his head. "I'm swimming out there."

"Seriously?"

"Yep. Just watch out for zombies for me, okay? Especially those two we just saw. They seem to be ignoring us for now, but that could change in a heartbeat."

"Yeah. No problem."

Bryce removed his socks and boots. "Okay, wish me luck."

"Good luck, man."

Bryce stepped into the water and swore under his breath. Even though it was in the middle of the summer, the river's water was still chilly.

"Cold?"

He waded further into the murky water. "Very," he said through clenched teeth. He then launched forward and began swimming toward the yacht, which was about three hundred yards away. He tried to ignore the smell of the water as it splashed against his face. Although he was no ecologist, he knew there was definitely something wrong with the river. Not only was it the wrong color, but it smelled like iron.

"Bryce!"

He stopped swimming and turned back to find both Billie and now Paige, both standing on the embankment, waving their arms frantically.

Dammit, he thought, planting his feet on a sandbank. *Why can't one of these girls just do what they're told for once!*

"Zombie!" hollered Billie.

Bryce turned around and found himself face to face with one. Gasping, he pulled his fist back and delivered a hard punch to the creature's nose, shattering any remaining bone and cartilage not yet decomposed. Then, before the zombie could retaliate, he threw himself back into the water and began swimming toward the boat once more. When he reached the back of the yacht, he climbed onto the swimming platform, took a few seconds to catch his breath, and then stepped onto the deck.

"Hello?" he called, knocking on the sliding glass door. When nobody answered, he pulled it open, stepped inside, and searched the impressive boat. Unfortunately, it appeared to have been abandoned.

Sighing, he turned to leave the galley when something caught his eye. A note taped to the refrigerator that said:

Went in search of supplies. If you are a stranger, please be respectful to our boat and we'll share what we have. If you're family, take off your shoes and stay awhile! We'll try to hurry - XOXO

Sighing, he rubbed a hand over his face, wondering what to do. They certainly couldn't wait around for Cassie's family to show up. It might not ever happen with all the shit going down.

Noticing the pen, he quickly scribbled a message of his own on the same note:

Cassie,
If you get this, we'll be at your grandparents' for the next couple of days. Come find us.
Love,
Bryce

Sighing, he walked out of the galley, through the boat's salon, and out the back, closing the sliding glass door. When he turned back around, he found himself looking right into a double-barreled shotgun.

14

ALLIE AND KYLIE

"Wait, you guys. I just can't walk any further,"
said Allie. "My feet are seriously killing me."

"We need to keep moving," said Justice,
turning around, walking backwards on the
pavement. "I think there's a house over that next
hill."

Her eyes narrowed. "You say that before every
hill."

The side of his lip went up. "One of these
times, I'll be right."

She stopped, took off her pink canvas shoes, and examined her heels in alarm. "See, they're both raw from blisters."

Justice walked back and stared at her ankles. "It's your own fault for wearing such cheap tennis shoes and no socks."

"It's not like I had a lot of choice in the matter," she muttered. "The only other ones I had were left in the truck we abandoned back at that parking ramp. The one *you* said was too dangerous to return to. So if anything, it's *your* fault."

"Well, it wasn't like I planned this hike," he said. "We just got stuck with the wrong truck."

"Hey, you guys, someone's coming!" cried Allie.

They both turned to stare at the large pair of headlights heading toward them in the distance.

"It's a semi," said Justice. "You girls get behind those trees over there. I'll see if they stop."

The girls ran toward the dark woods and hid behind a large oak tree as the truck got closer. When it slowed down and finally came to a stop, Justice walked up to it.

"Hey, kid," smiled the passenger, a man who looked to be in his late twenties. "You need a ride?"

The dark-haired man had a friendly enough smile but there was something about him that seemed off.

"Maybe. Where you heading?" asked Justice.

"Oh, here and there," he replied, scratching his scruffy chin. "What about you?"

"Minnesota."

"You have a long way to go."

Justice chuckled. "Tell me about it."

"Well, you're in luck because we'll be passing through that way. Have some business to take care of in Canada. You may as well join us."

"You don't mind?" asked Justice.

"Hell no," said the man. "In fact, it's your lucky day, kid. We've got space as well as food and water. That's why we're using this rig." He grinned and patted the outside of the door. "It came fully supplied with life's little necessities."

Truth be told, he *was* parched and the thought of water made his mouth feel even drier. "So, what about your friend in the cab – he okay with this? Sharing a ride and some of your supplies with a stranger?"

The man turned to the driver and said something, then turned back. "He said to get in, time's a-wasting."

Justice turned toward the woods, wondering if he was making the right choice. Plus, they still didn't know about the girls.

"Your friends are also welcome," said the driver, leaning over to the open window. He smiled warmly. "We have plenty to spare and would be honored if you'd all joined us."

He stared back at the red-haired man and wondered how he'd known about the girls.

***

Five minutes later, Justice sat between the two men while the girls rode in the back sleeping compartment.

"So, what's your name?" asked the dark-haired man, who was a lot bigger than Justice had originally thought.

"Justice."

"I'm Travis," said the driver. "And that's Dwayne. Glad you could join us."

"Uh, sure. Thanks for inviting us."

"So, where'd you hook up with those two girls?" asked Dwayne, his eyes glittering with a little too much interest for a man his age.

Justice's eyes narrowed when he noticed Dwayne's teardrop tattoo. Having spent time in a tattoo shop, he was well aware of the symbolism of Dwayne's tattoo. "Met them a few towns back. When did you get the tat?"

"Which one?" he chuckled, raising the bottom of his T-shirt until his inked torso was exposed. He had dozens of them – from dragons and skulls, to pierced hearts and black roses.

"I was talking about the one under your eye."

Dwayne sighed. "Well, got that one a while back."

"You kill someone?"

"Now, if I asked you that question right now, I am pretty sure we'd both have the same answer."

"The people I kill are already dead," said Justice.

He chuckled. "Well, the ones I've killed should have been."

"Don't worry about him," interrupted Travis. "He won't kill unless instructed to."

Instructed to?

Justice tried to remain calm. "Oh, yeah?"

"Yes, his priorities have been," he smiled, "adjusted."

"Oh, well, *that's* refreshing," he answered. *This conversation was both disturbing and crazy*, he thought.

"Now, Justice, don't get yourself all flustered. I have no issues with you at the moment. In fact, I believe you could be very helpful in our mission," said Travis.

"Ah... what kind of a mission are we talking about, besides staying alive?"

"It's a little complicated," he answered. "And, I don't think you're quite ready to appreciate the enormity of our plans or your possible involvement. But something tells me you'll step up to the plate when... properly persuaded."

He frowned. "Is that right?"

Travis smiled darkly. "Oh, yes. We've been watching you, Justice. You're a good soldier, very dependable. The way you risked your life to help those two girls in the parking ramp. My master was quite impressed with your determination and fighting skills."

"Your master? And... what the hell? Were you watching us?" asked Justice, tensing up. "You could have offered to help out a little if that was really the case."

Travis laid a hand on his forearm. "Calm down," he said in a hypnotically smooth voice. "Or you'll scare your friends in the back. You don't want that now, do you?"

Justice felt a strong wave of nausea and his lungs felt as if all the air had been sucked out. He attempted to pull his arm away from Travis's firm grasp, but instead found himself immobile.

"Your fear," hissed Travis, his eyes turning a golden-red hue, "is... intoxicating, I must admit. I wonder how exhilarating it would be if I were to tear the three of you from limb to limb, starting with the lovely little girls in back? Let you listen to their terrified screams and watch all of that sweet agony, all the while knowing that you're next... hmm?"

Horrified, Justice tried to speak, but couldn't move his mouth.

Travis went on, his strange eyes dancing with delight. "It would be quite fun for me, I assure you, but fortunately for you, we need you to help our cause."

It was then that Justice noticed the truck was still moving forward on the road, on its own, without any help from Travis.

Who was this guy?

"Oh, I am one of your worst nightmares," said Travis. "That's all you need to know."

I still don't understand, thought Justice, staring in terror at Travis's glowing eyes – they seemed to penetrate into his very soul. *And why does he need me?*

Because you're an atheist, proclaimed the amused voice in his head, *and we really like those.*

15

The nuns had generously offered us food, bottled water, and blankets for our journey. We had just finished loading the Honda with the items when I felt as if I was forgetting something else. I closed my eyes and did a mental list of what we'd need and what *might* still be missing, but just couldn't put my finger on it.

"You're leaving?"

I opened my eyes and turned around to find Kallie staring up at me with tears in her blue eyes.

"Yes," I said, feeling a tug at my heart. I bent down on one knee. "I have to go look for my grandparents, and Nora needs to find her father."

"Take me with you," she pleaded, throwing her arms around me. "I'll be good. I promise!"

I closed my eyes and hugged her back. "I can't, honey," I said, now feeling choked up myself. "It's too dangerous out there for you. Heck, it's too dangerous for us."

"But you can't leave me!" she cried, pulling away. "What if my mother wants to hug me, again?"

I groaned inwardly – me and my bright ideas. I shouldn't have ever mentioned her mother. "Kallie, if your mother wants to hug you, she will. Whether it's in the form of Sister Theresa or any one of the other nuns, you will get that hug. She doesn't need me to do it."

"But I felt something special when you hugged me! I've never felt that way with anyone else. You have to take me with you, Cassie. Please!"

Sister Francine stepped behind the young girl and put a hand on her shoulder. "Now, Kallie, you have to let Cassie get ready for her trip."

"But she's has to take me with her!" she cried, clutching me tighter.

"I just can't, Kallie. It's not safe."

"What's going on over here?" asked Henry, chewing on some kind of beef stick.

"Someone wants to come with," I said, looking up at him.

His eyes softened. "Looks like you've made quite the impression here, Wild."

I smiled. "Looks like."

"You know, when we come back this way, we could pick her up and take her back to the hotel with us. There's plenty of room. Hell, Belinda always wanted a little girl of her own – we'll bring her back as a gift."

"Oh, Henry. She isn't a doll," sighed the nun. "She's a little girl who needs a family, a real family."

His eyebrows furrowed. "Sister, as far as I'm concerned, we *are* a real family. A little unconventional, but we all look out for each other, try our best to keep one another safe. Seems to me this little girl has taken a fancy to one of our own, and obviously, vice-versa. It would be a shame to cause any more sorrow or pain in Kallie's life, don't you think?"

"Well, we all just want what's best for her," she replied.

"Well, good. Then, it's settled. We'll be picking her up on our way from Minnesota within the next week."

"Did you hear that, Kallie?" I murmured, "We'll be coming back for you real soon."

She pulled away and stared into my eyes. "You promise?"

"I promise," I said.

"You shouldn't make promises you might not be able to keep," said the nun, after Kallie had skipped off to tell her friends. "What if something happens to you?"

"Sister," said Henry. "I'm surprised. Aren't you the ones always encouraging others to have faith?"

She smiled. "Well, I guess you've got me there."

16

"Whoa," said Bryce, raising his hands. "I'm friend, not foe. In fact, I know the Wild family."

"Oh, sorry," said the man, smiling broadly as he lowered the gun. "Wasn't sure if you were here to steal from us or what your deal was. Name's Tom," he said, holding out his hand. "Tom Jones."

"Bryce De Luca," he answered, shaking it.

"So, kid, what are you doing out here?"

"Well, looking for Cassie and her grandparents, Steve and Irene Wild."

"Unfortunately, they've left the city," said Tom. "At least, Steve and Irene. I'm not sure about Cassie, haven't seen her for a long time."

"Where did Steve and Irene go?"

He sighed. "Well, they heard from their son Dave a couple of weeks ago and left for Atlanta – when the cell phones were still working. Haven't seen anyone since."

Bryce's stomach dropped – they could be anywhere.

If they were still alive.

"Tom!" hollered a woman's voice.

"It's all right, Barb! He knows the Wilds!" called Tom, leaning over the side of the boat.

Seconds later, a dark-haired woman climbed out of a battered, fiberglass canoe and onto the yacht. "Well," she grinned, setting her oversized bag onto the deck. "We don't get very many visitors, unless they're dead and inviting themselves to dinner."

"I bet. In fact, I met one on my way out here," said Bryce. "Have either of you noticed how the zombies have started entering all of the lakes and rivers?"

"Yeah. Started a couple of days ago. Something seems to be drawing them in," said Tom.

"Something, as in 'blood'," said Barb.

"Oh, Barb," sighed Tom.

"Oh, Barb nothing. The water is turning into blood." She turned to Bryce. "Tom here doesn't want to believe it, though. Thinks *I'm* going crazy."

"I never said that. I just don't think we should start packing it in because the water looks a little different."

"I'm with you, Tom," said Bryce. "I'm sure there's a logical explanation."

"Okay, be stubborn, both of you. But I've already told you what I think, Tom. Don't go discounting it just because it sounds inconceivable. The fact that there are zombies walking this planet reminds us that nothing is implausible."

"I know."

The couple stared at each other silently, an unspoken message passing between them.

"It smells funny, too," said Barb, turning back to Bryce. "The water."

Bryce nodded. "I know. I had to swim in it."

"So, what are you going to do, young man?" asked Tom. "Do you have somewhere to go?"

"Yeah, after we find Cassie and her sister, we'll be heading back to Atlanta."

Barb's eyes widened. "What do you mean? They're lost?"

Bryce went over everything that had happened with the Wilds, including the death of Dave and Kris.

Barb's hand flew to her mouth. "Oh, my God," she moaned. "Steve and Irene are going to be devastated."

Bryce nodded. "It was a horrible experience for everyone, especially the girls."

"How are they handling it?" she asked.

"Well, they're handling it because they have no choice. Fortunately, both of them are pretty tough girls."

Barb smiled sadly. "Yes, they certainly are. Well, I'll say a prayer that you'll all be reunited soon."

"Thanks," he said, staring off into the distance.

Tom sighed. "What a nightmare, huh? Sometimes I feel like none of this is real."

"I wish that's all it was," replied Bryce. "Just a really bad dream."

"So, you still think Cassie is headed out this way?" asked Tom.

"Not sure anymore. Hell, for all I know, she hasn't even made it to her grandparents' yet. I'm hoping when I get back there, she'll be waiting."

"You'll find them, son. I have a feeling it won't be long now."

"Hope you're right." Lightning lit up the sky and Bryce frowned. "Well, I suppose I'd better get back. My buddy is still waiting for me on shore and is probably mad as hell because of who he's babysitting."

"Babysitting?" asked Barb.

Bryce smirked. "Oh, nothing. Inside joke. Anyway, are you guys interested in returning to Atlanta with us?"

Tom put his arm around Barb. "We're going to take our chances here. If what you're saying is correct, the road is dangerous, and it isn't much better in Atlanta than it is here."

"But you won't be alone," said Bryce. "You'd be with other survivors, including your friends."

"It's very nice of you to invite us," said Barb. "But Tom is right – we're going to hang here. It's the only place that feels normal and we really need that."

Bryce nodded. "Well, I guess I can appreciate that. If you change your mind, though, we'll be hanging out at Steven and Irene's home for a week or two, unless everyone shows up earlier. Otherwise, we're staying at the Ritz Carlton in Atlanta beyond that."

"Thanks, Bryce," said Tom. "We'll keep that in mind."

He climbed back down to the swimming platform. "Well, wish me luck," he said, then dove into the water.

"Good luck!" they yelled after he resurfaced. He waved and then started swimming back to the shoreline as the rain began to pick up again. When he reached the spot he'd left Billie, it was deserted. Thinking they left to get out of the rain, he quickly put his boots and shirt back on, and then headed back toward the truck.

17

ALLIE AND KYLIE

"Something's wrong," whispered Kylie.

Allie yawned and stretched her arms. "What do you mean?"

"Nobody up front has talked or said anything for the last couple of hours. It's so quiet... it's eerie."

They were still in the sleeper compartment, which was separated from the truck's cab by a curtain. Allie crawled over to the curtain and peeked around it.

"Justice is sleeping in the middle," she said, lying back down. "The other two guys aren't really saying a word to each other," she said to Kylie.

"It's kind of weird, isn't it?"

Allie shrugged. "I don't know, guys don't usually have as much to say as we do."

"Hello, ladies," said Dwayne, sticking his head through the curtain. "Have a good rest?"

"Yes," they answered in unison.

He smiled. "Good. We'll be stopping soon, so you can stretch your legs."

"Thanks," answered Allie.

"Um, is Justice still sleeping?" asked Kylie.

He hesitated. "Yes, but I'm sure he'll be waking up soon."

"Are we almost to Minnesota?" asked Allie.

"Almost. You excited to see your sister?"

Allie nodded.

"Good. Now, just hold tight and we'll let you know when we get to our first destination."

"Where is that?" asked Allie.

"You'll see. It's a surprise, actually. A place in Minnesota you're both very familiar with."

"Oh, okay," said Allie.

Dwayne closed the curtain and Kylie turned to Allie. "Is it me, or is that guy seriously creepy?"

She nodded. "Yes. Did you see that tattoo on his eye? I think it's some gang thing."

"You think he's in a gang?"

Allie snorted. "Hello? Just look at him. He's got that long-haired hippie thing going on, has tattoos, and wears a jean vest. Guys in jean vests are almost always in gangs. Haven't you ever watched *Sons of Anarchy*?"

"No."

"Well, take it from me, they both belong to some type of gang and I'm sure they're dangerous. We should watch them closely."

"Justice wouldn't let them do anything to harm anyone," she said. "He's looking out for us now."

"I hope so," said Allie.

***

Two hours later, the semi came to a stop.

"We're here," said Travis, opening up the curtain.

"Thank goodness," said Allie, laying her hand down. They'd been playing cards for the past hour and she'd lost interest in them forty-five minutes ago.

"What's wrong with Justice?" asked Kylie, noticing that his head was still slumped forward in sleep.

Travis turned and laid a hand on Justice, whose head immediately lifted. "Wake up, son," he said. "We've arrived."

Justice nodded and mumbled something incoherent.

"Oh, my God!" cried Allie, looking over Justice's shoulder at the view outside of the truck. "I never thought I'd see this place again."

"What?" asked Kylie, moving in beside her. She leaned forward and smiled sadly. "Oh."

"The Mall of America," said Travis, as they stared at the entrance to the massive structure. "What a tragedy, huh?"

What was once an impressive infrastructure and one of the world's largest malls in the world, was now just another victim in the zombie apocalypse. Glass doors were smashed, graffiti graced much of the outside walls, garbage, and what looked like human remains, lined the white sidewalks.

"It's horrible," shuddered Kylie, remembering how thrilling the mega-mall had seemed when she was little – especially the indoor amusement park, the numerous toy stores, and mouthwatering candy shops. Now, she'd never get a chance to try out the new rollercoaster or see another movie in the mall's theater. Nothing would ever be the same. Not here or anywhere else, for that matter.

"Shall we get out of the truck?" asked Travis.

"What are we doing here?" asked Allie. "Getting supplies?"

"That, among other things," said Dwayne with sly grin on his face."

"What's going on?" asked Kylie. "I thought you were going to bring us to Wolf Creek?"

"All in good time. First we have a very important meeting to attend," said Travis, leaving the truck.

"A meeting? With whom?" asked Allie after she and Kylie jumped down from the cab.

"With others who want to join our cause," smiled Travis. "You're certainly invited. In fact, I insist that you come. It will be fairly enlightening."

The girls looked at each other in confusion and then turned back to him. "I'm not sure what *cause* you're talking about, but we really can't stay," said Allie. "We have to go find my sister as soon as possible. Is there any way that either of you could drive us to Wolf Creek?"

"Certainly," said Dwayne. "Later."

"When later?" she asked.

"After the meeting is over. After midnight."

"But that's too late!" Allie hurried over to Justice, who still looked disoriented and confused. "Justice, can you get us to my grandparents' house sooner? Please? Maybe you can hotwire another car or something?" she said, looking around. They'd parked in a lot across from Nordstrom's and there were plenty of abandoned vehicles to choose from.

He didn't respond. Instead, he raised his hands and began staring at them as if he'd never seen them before.

"Uh, Justice?" she tried again, stepping closer. "Are you okay?"

"He's fine," said Travis, placing a hand on Justice's back. "Just needs a little more fresh air. Isn't that right, kid?"

"Yes," said Justice, dropping his hands. "I just need a little more fresh air."

"Okay, *then* can you help us?" asked Kylie.

Justice looked at Travis, who shook his head.

Allie scowled. "What's happening here? Why are you acting so weird?"

"We can't leave," answered Justice, his eyes still transfixed on Travis. "I'm needed here."

Frantic, Allie grabbed ahold of his arms and tried shaking him. "What in the world is wrong with you?"

Justice tilted his head and stared at her in confusion, his eyes dilated. "I'm needed here."

"Oh, my God!" cried Kylie, pointing toward the road. "Zombies!"

Allie turned and gasped in shock.

"Ah, yes," smiled Travis, nodding his head. "Some of the guests have already begun to arrive."

The girls watched in horror as hundreds of zombies, in all of their decomposed glory, trudged through the streets toward them.

"We've got to get out of here!" hollered Allie, backing toward the semi. "Come on, you guys!"

"Relax," said Travis, turning to her. "You have nothing to fear."

"Uh, yes we do!" she cried. "And so do you!"

Kylie grabbed Justice's arm and tugged. "Come on!"

He ignored her and watched the zombies creep closer.

"Justice!" she yelled. "They're coming! You have no chance surviving that mob! Seriously!"

Still, he did not respond, nor did he make any move to follow her.

"They're glorious, aren't they?" smiled Travis, with a satisfied grin.

Kylie turned to him in disbelief. "Glorious? What are you talking about?"

"My soldiers. They're almost perfect, actually."

Believing that Travis had gone completely mad, Kylie tried one more time to pull Justice toward the truck, but he wouldn't move.

"Come on!" hollered Allie, opening the semi door. "If he's not joining us, there's nothing more you can do. He'll just have to take care of himself!"

"But –"

"Kylie! Look, he's not listening to you and he's obviously not going anywhere, but you have to! You can't fight those things!"

"Justice!" sobbed Kylie. "Get into the truck!"

"Let him be," said Travis, pulling her away. "He will not be persuaded."

Kylie backed away and then quickly got into the truck with Allie.

Allie stared down at the three men incredulously. "What are you doing?" she screamed, through the window. "They're going to kill you all!"

"Justice!" moaned Kylie, tears running down her cheek. "What's wrong with you?"

The three men ignored the girls and watched as the zombies moved closer, making their familiar guttural noises. When they were less than twenty feet away, however, the zombies stopped moving and everything became silent.

Dead silent.

"Good!" hollered Travis after a few seconds. Then he walked back to the semi and climbed onto the hood of the truck until he was standing and facing the crowd. He raised his hands and smiled down at the horror that was watching him with attentiveness. "Yes, indeed, this is very good."

18

Nora finally took out her dad's CD and we listened to it as we resumed our journey back to Minnesota. She sat in the front, staring out the window while Henry drove, his hands clutching the steering wheel so tightly, that I thought he worried the heavy metal music would somehow shake him off. He was a trooper, however, and didn't complain, although I was sure the music was driving him crazy. When the last song ended, Henry removed the CD and handed it back to Nora.

"What did you think?" she asked him, trying to bite back a smile.

He cleared his throat. "Well, it was *loud*."

She chuckled. "Yeah, I know. Not your type of music."

"Well, now, I never said I didn't like it. Fact is, I'm pretty hip about a lot of things."

Nora and I both burst out laughing.

"What's so funny?" he asked, his watery blue eyes twinkling.

"Hip?" I chuckled, still laughing at the old term. "Oh, come on, Henry. Wasn't it just yesterday that you were complaining about the horrible music being made these days?"

"I will have you know that just because I'm seventy-five years old doesn't mean my mind isn't open to change or new ideas, Wild."

"Now, Henry," I said, "I thought you were eighty-something?"

He scowled. "Never assume anything. Didn't I teach you that?" Henry reached into his pocket and pulled out his tin of chew. "Besides, eighty is the new seventy, Wild. Haven't you heard?"

"Oh, of course."

"So you really liked the CD?" asked Nora.

He shoved a wad of chew into his mouth. "No."

"What did you think?" she asked, turning to look back at me.

"He's very talented," I said, although thrash metal wasn't really my type of music, either.

She turned back around. "He's more talented at making music than being a father," she said softly.

Nora had told me once that her grandfather had died when her father had been very young, and they'd been very close. His death had almost destroyed the eight-year-old boy at the time.

"Maybe it had something to do with his dad dying so young. You said it messed him up pretty bad," I said, putting my hand on her shoulder.

She stiffened up.

"Sorry," I said, removing it.

"It's okay," she replied, turning back around. "I'm just kind of tense right now."

"I understand," I said. We were all pretty stressed out and on the edge.

"So, Nora, where do you think we might find your father?" asked Henry, opening his window.

"We should check my grandmother's house," she said. "I left him a note a few weeks ago. Said

I'd try making it back there and that he should leave me a message if he made it."

Henry spit out his wad of chew. "Sounds like a good plan. Wild, what about your grandparents?"

"We need to drive out to their house, see if they're there."

"You haven't spoken to them since this mess started?" he asked.

"No. We tried calling them but they never answered their cell phone. My dad had told me they'd gotten the flu shot this year and I actually think he was afraid to search for them. If they would have been zombies..."

Henry nodded. "I know he wouldn't have been able to shoot them. Sometimes it's better to *not* know."

"So, why are we searching for them if they had the flu shot?" asked Nora.

"Well, Allie and I both survived getting bitten by zombies. They might be immune to the virus as well."

"What are you going to do if we find them and they're not who you think they are anymore?" asked Henry.

My grandparents were kind and loving people. There was one thing I knew for certain – they'd rather die than hurt another living soul.

I sighed. "Lay them to rest."

***

A couple hours later, we entered Minnesota and my heart began to race.

We were so close.

"Where should we go first?" asked Henry.

"Nora's grandmother's house," I said, watching the raindrops on the windshield. Since the trip had been her idea, it was only right.

"You sure?" she asked.

"Yep. Let's go find your dad before we lose him again."

She nodded. "Thanks, Wild."

"Don't thank me. This entire road trip was your idea and I should be thanking you, especially if we find my grandparents alive."

"If they're alive, we'll find them," said Nora. "We won't stop looking for them, either."

I smiled.

"You guys want to listen to my dad's CD again?" asked Nora.

"No!" both Henry and I answered in unison.

She chuckled. "You guys are wimps," she said, playing with the dials. When she pushed the FM button by accident, we heard a man's deep voice being broadcasted over the airwaves. We stared at each other in shock and turned up the volume.

"The time has come for the remaining survivors to form a stronghold against the zombies. We need to band together and take back what is ours," he said. "So if you're out there, find us, and join us."

"Yeah but where are you?" whispered Nora.

The man kept talking about having a generous food and water supply that they were willing to share as well, if and when other survivors showed up to join their cause.

"Get on with it," mumbled Henry. "Can't find you if you don't tell us where you're at."

Then, as if the man had heard him, he announced where their bunker was.

My jaw dropped.

"The Mall of America," said Nora, turning down the radio. "How in the world could anyone secure that place? There are too many doorways. They'd have to kill all the zombies and then board up every one of those glass doorways."

"Anything is possible," said Henry. "Besides, most of the zombies were sick people before they turned. Probably weren't many of them hanging out at the mall with the flu."

"Yeah, right. My sister wouldn't let a little vomiting or fever keep her from shopping if she had the money and the vehicle to get her there. I'll bet there were plenty of zombies wandering the mall before these guys secured it," I said.

"This is good news," said Nora. "If we can't find our relatives at their homes, there may be a chance they've joined this Minnesota survivor's group."

"You might be right," said Henry. "But it still sounds a little too good to be true."

"I know. But at least we have another place to check if we can't find our families," I said.

"Damn tootin'. Plus, I could use me a new change of clothes if we do make it to this mall. The ones I'm wearing are about ready to get up and walk away on their own."

"Yeah," said Nora. "You're starting to smell as bad as the zombies."

"It's all a part of my camouflage," smiled Henry. "Blend in with their smell and they can't even tell I'm alive. Hell, I've got one foot in the grave as it is."

"Oh brother," sighed Nora.

I shook his shoulder playfully. "You do not have one foot in the grave. Quit talking that way."

"I tell you one thing," said Henry. "Dying doesn't scare me anymore, Wild. Dying before I have the chance to get you girls safely back to Atlanta, now that's what scares the tar out of me. I don't want to let you down."

"You could never let us down," I said. "Now quit talking about dying."

"Well, I just want you both to know, I've got your backs."

"We've got yours, too," I said.

He nodded but said nothing more, which was a relief, because this melancholy side of him made me feel guilty. Back at the hotel, he'd obviously felt secure and happy for the first time in weeks. But then he'd decided to be a hero, just to keep the two of us safe from harm. If anything happened to him, I'd never forgive myself, and either would Nora.

"Thanks, Henry," I said.

"For what?" he asked, glancing at me in his rearview mirror.

"Everything. For being there for me every time I've needed you. Starting from that very first time we met. When I rear-ended you."

His eyes sparkled. "Too bad I couldn't have been there for you when you were learning how to drive."

19

When Bryce made it back to the marina, Paige and Billie were nowhere to be found.

"Billie!" he hollered, stepping away from the SUV. "Paige!"

He heard a faint cry on the other side of the marina where some of the larger boats were docked, and immediately took off toward the sound. When he arrived, he found Paige, Billie, and a dead woman's bloody corpse lying nearby.

"Thank God," cried Paige, who was crouched down next to Billie.

"What happened?!" hollered Bryce, rushing over to him. "Oh shit, were you bit?"

He was lying on his side with blood seeping out of a wound on his neck. "Yeah," he whispered in a hoarse voice.

Bryce took off his T-shirt and pressed it against Billie's neck. He looked at Paige. "What happened to him?"

She swallowed. "When you were on the boat, about five zombies appeared out of nowhere, surprised the crap out of us. I think they were heading toward the river like the other ones, you know? Anyway, we ran away from them and back here. Then, when we were about to get back into the SUV, Billie thought he heard a baby crying so we both rushed over here."

"Zombies?"

"Yeah, well, two of them were on this woman," she said, her eyes full of tears. "It was," she shuddered, "horrible and too late, you know?"

"So, how did they get Billie?"

"Well, he slipped on the wet dock and they..." she closed her eyes and began to cry, "they pounced on him before he could shoot or I could do anything to stop them."

"What happened to the zombies?" he asked, looking around.

"I... I... killed them," she said, opening her eyes. "And pushed them into the water."

"It's so hot," whispered Billie, his face pale. "My skin feels like it's on fire."

"You're going to be okay," said Bryce, forcing a smile. "We're going to bring you back with us and get this little wound of yours taken care of. It's really not that bad."

"No," whispered Billie, grabbing Bryce's wrist. "Too... dangerous. I can already feel the virus spreading through my veins."

"Don't argue," said Bryce. "You're going to be fine. Cassie beat this thing, and so will you."

Billie's eyes began to close. "Save the baby," he whispered.

Bryce's eyebrows shot up. "Baby, what baby?"

"On the boat..."

"Hold this," he said to Paige, motioning toward the shirt.

She nodded and took over while Bryce stood up and walked toward the Carver.

"I don't think there's a baby around here, guys," said Bryce, climbing onto the deck.

And that's when they both heard it, a faint cry from somewhere inside the cabin.

Bryce opened up the door and disappeared inside. Seconds later he reappeared, his face full of shock. In his arms was a bundle of what was obviously more than just a pile of blankets.

"Oh, my God," gasped Paige, when the baby began to cry, its little arms flailing angrily.

Bryce sighed. "Yeah. A baby."

"Crap, what are we going to do?"

"I'm going to give you the baby and make sure you two get back to the vehicle safely. Then I'll come back for Billie, before the rain gets any worse."

"Is it safe?" she asked, staring down at Billie.

Bryce's lips thinned. "I don't know. But we just can't *leave* him. He's alive right now. Plus, he's one of us. We're not leaving anyone behind."

"You could tie him up somehow," said Paige standing.

He smiled grimly. "Good thinking."

She held out her arms and Bryce placed the infant into them. "Oh," she smiled, staring down at the small baby, who couldn't have been more than a couple months old, "she's so sweet."

"How do you know it's a she?" asked Bryce, kneeling down next to Billie.

Paige kissed the baby's forehead. "Because," she said, softening her voice, "she obviously cries when you hold her and now that I've got her, she's content. You have that effect on women."

Bryce rolled his eyes.

"See, she's smiling at me," said Paige.

"What do we need for the baby?" he asked. "Don't babies need diapers and milk or something?"

"Diapers and formula," said Paige. "We're going to have to pick some up somewhere."

"I'll search the boat after everyone is safe. Let's get you both to the SUV first."

They were back on the road thirty minutes later, with Billie restrained in the back with buoy rope.

"They had a first-aid kit," said Bryce. "I put some iodine on his neck and bandaged it up. He's got a fever, though, and I couldn't find any aspirin."

"What about things for the baby?"

"Well, there was only a handful of diapers and I couldn't find any formula on the boat. We're still going to have to stop somewhere."

"We need a car seat, too," said Paige, staring down at the baby, who was sleeping. "It's against the law to be traveling like this."

Bryce snorted. "What law?"

"I know, but we still need it. It's safer."

They found a small grocery store on the edge of town, which appeared quiet and free of zombies.

"Stay out here with her. I'll be back," said Bryce, grabbing the gun.

"What if he changes into a zombie?" she whispered.

"He's tied up. Even if he does, he can't get to you."

Paige sighed. "Poor Billie."

"He might make it through this. Don't give up hope just yet."

"God, I hope you're right."

"I'll get some peroxide for his wound and more bandages. Obviously they won't have any car seats, but they'll hopefully have formula."

"We can always find another vehicle with a car seat," she said, looking hopeful.

"Keep a lookout for one then."

Bryce got out of the SUV and Paige watched as he ran into the store through the rain. Unfortunately, even from this distance, she could tell that the place had already been ransacked by other survivors. She hoped none of them had babies.

"What's your name, little one?" she whispered, staring down at the sleeping baby. "I guess you're too young to tell me."

"Paige," mumbled Billie, from the back.

She stiffened up. "Uh, yeah, Billie?"

"Why are my hands tied?"

"You were bit by a zombie, remember?"

He didn't say anything.

"Billie?"

"Yeah."

"Are you okay?"

"I've felt better."

"Um, you were right about the baby."

"What baby?" he asked, struggling to sit up.

She turned around. "The baby on the boat. Don't you remember?"

"No."

The only thing he could remember was getting bitten by the zombie and then the intense heat.

Even now he could still feel the fire raging through his veins.

"You don't look so good."

"I feel like shit. Do you have any water?"

"No, but we're at a grocery store. Bryce should be back in a few minutes."

Billie turned and stared at the building. "He went in alone?"

"Well, I certainly couldn't go in with the baby."

"You could have left the baby in here."

Not with you, she thought. After what had happened to Austin, there was no way she was going to take any chances around Billie.

"Looks like he found what we needed," she said, relieved to see Bryce leaving the store with a large box of diapers and a bag.

"Hey, bro," said Bryce, opening up the back of the SUV. "How are you feeling?"

"Not good."

"Fortunately for you, I found some pain medication and a bottle of seltzer water. Everything else was pretty much picked over by looters."

"Looks like the looters didn't need diapers," said Paige.

"Or formula," said Bryce, setting down the bag. "I wasn't sure which kind to get so I grabbed a couple different kinds along with some plastic bottles. Oh, and wet-wipes."

Paige glanced down at the baby, who was beginning to get restless. "Um, I have a feeling we're going to need a lot of things. Things we're forgetting. Well, my mom will know what to do once we get the baby back to her."

"I'm sure you're right," said Bryce. "I still remember when Bobby was a baby, seems like we went through diapers and formula like water. Speaking of which, I did find some distilled water in the back of the store. I'll have to go back for it."

"Bryce, you gotta untie me, man."

He sighed. "I just can't. It's for everyone's safety."

"Dammit, I'm not turning into one of *them*," he snapped. "Take off the rope!"

Paige and Bryce looked at each other. It was obvious that Billie was already showing signs of aggression.

"Settle down. We have to wait until we get back to the house," said Bryce.

Billie clenched his jaw. "This is bullshit."

"Sorry. Here," he said, opening up the bottle of pills. "Take a couple of these and try to sleep. Your body needs it."

"Fine," said Billie, opening up his mouth.

Bryce quickly pushed the pills in and then opened up the seltzer water. "You're going to be all right."

"She's getting mad up here," said Paige as the baby began to fret. "We need to mix some formula."

Bryce nodded. "Okay," I'll be back." Then he closed the back of the SUV and ran back toward the store.

"Paige," said Billie. "I have to pee."

"Why didn't you tell Bryce when he was still here?"

"Because I wasn't thinking about it at the time."

"Sorry, you're going to have to hold it."

"Thanks."

"What the heck do you want me to do about it?" she snapped back. "I have to take care of… Adria here."

"Adria?"

"Yeah, the baby. She needs a name and that one seems to suit her," she said, staring into the baby's blue eyes. A smile spread across her plump cheeks and Paige grinned back. "I think you like that name, don't you, sweetie?"

"Paige, I really need to go."

"Bryce will be back in a flash. Hold it."

"Jesus, you two are both being totally unreasonable."

She turned back. "No, you are. You'd do the same thing in our position. I mean, seriously, you're being irrational right now."

Billie didn't reply, he just laid his head against the back window and stared out into the night.

The rain began to pick up again as Bryce pushed a cart filled with five jugs of water toward the SUV.

"Billie has to pee," said Paige, when he opened the back.

Bryce sighed. "Okay. Let me load this stuff and then I'll help you."

"Just untie me and I'll do it myself," said Billie.

"We already went through this," replied Bryce.

"Dude, you're not going to help me pee. It's just not going to happen."

Bryce sighed. "Yeah, I guess you're right. Look, I'll untie you for this but after that, we have to restrain you again."

"Fine," said Billie, glaring at him.

Bryce pulled out his knife and began cutting Billie's rope. "Good thing I brought extra."

"Bryce! Look out behind you!" yelled Paige.

Two zombies were staggering toward him in the parking lot. He quickly turned around and rushed the zombies, stabbing the first one in the head. Before he could get to the second one, Billie appeared by his side with a long wrench and smashed it against the zombie's skull.

"Thanks," said Bryce, as the zombie slumped forward.

"See, if I was turning into one of these, I'd be going after you and not those zombies."

"Right. Uh, why don't you go behind that car and pee while I get the formula to Paige."

Billie nodded and walked away.

"What do you think?" asked Paige, when Bryce got back to the SUV. "Is it safe to let him go unrestrained?"

"I don't know. Probably not."

When Billie made it back to the truck, he ignored the trunk compartment and sat behind Paige. "Let's go."

Bryce sighed. "We have to tie you up, man. Sorry."

"No. I'm not going to agree to that. Either you trust me or leave me the hell here."

Bryce and Paige looked at each other.

"For the love of God, just relax. I'm not going to bite you guys. Aren't you the one that said Cassie pulled through?"

"Yeah, but Eva didn't," said Paige. "And either did Austin. Both of them became hostile and angry. Kind of like you're doing right now, Billie."

He smiled humorlessly. "Wow, Paige. Thanks for stomping out any bright hope I may have had for my future."

"Well, it's the truth," she mumbled.

Bryce rubbed his forehead. "Look, fine, we'll keep you untied. But if you feel like you're losing your grip on reality, let us know, will you?"

Billie snorted and then looked out the window. "I've felt like that before any zombie ever got to me."

"How's your neck feeling?" asked Bryce, starting the engine.

"It still hurts like a son-of-a-bitch. But it's a little more manageable now that the pills are kicking in."

"Good," he replied.

"You never told us what happened on the yacht," said Paige.

He pulled out of the parking lot and zigzagged around a couple of zombies. "They weren't there, but some friends of theirs were."

"Did they happen to tell you where Steve and Irene are?" she asked.

He ran a hand through his wet hair. "Yeah, they left for Atlanta about three weeks ago."

"No shit?" asked Billie.

"No shit. This entire trip is basically a waste of time."

"Only if Nora doesn't find her father," said Billie.

"Exactly," he replied. "Let's hope she does."

20

"How is Travis *doing* all of this?" asked Allie, staring out the window of the semi as more zombies arrived to join the others. "And what in the heck is wrong with Justice?"

"I have no idea," said Kylie. "But there's one thing for certain…"

"We're not in Kansas anymore?"

"That and we're in a crap-load of trouble. This guy is obviously dangerous. I actually think that he has some kind of hypnotic power over the zombies and Justice."

"He must, but how could he?"

"I don't know. Maybe he's not human."

Allie smiled humorlessly. "Maybe he's some kind of angel who's come to save us all from the zombies."

"Or maybe he's from the other place and wants to take over the world."

Allie started laughing but stopped when she noticed that Kylie was serious. The hair stood up on the back of her neck as she thought about everything that had happened in the last few weeks.

Obviously, at this point, anything was possible.

"So, um, you really think he's the Devil or something?"

"I… don't know, maybe," she said, her eyes full of fear.

"He's been nice, though. I mean if he was Satan, wouldn't he have tried killing us or something?"

"Or, he'd try to use us somehow," whispered Kylie, as if Travis could actually hear them from outside.

"Not me," she whispered back. "I won't let him."

They stared at Travis, who was still talking to the zombies, although they couldn't hear what he was saying. They'd shut the windows when the stench of the dead had become too much to handle.

Allie licked her lips. "Kylie, how are we going to get out of here?"

"I don't know."

"I wonder if we could sneak away while the zombies are like this? They seem really into what Travis is saying."

"I can't believe they're actually listening to him."

"I know, but seriously, now would be a good time to leave."

"I don't know if we should take that chance. Plus, we can't leave Justice."

"Justice has obviously left the building."

"No, I think if we can just get him alone, we can bring him back to reality," said Kylie.

"I hope so."

Just then, Travis stopped talking and the zombies began to disperse.

"What's going on now?" whispered Allie, as Travis climbed off of the truck. "Where are they going?"

"I don't know."

Travis opened the passenger door of the truck and smiled. "Time to get out, ladies."

"Um, we'd like to stay inside, if you don't mind," said Kylie.

He stared at them for a few seconds and then nodded. "If that's what you want."

"How did you do that?" sputtered Allie.

His eyes twinkled. "Do what?"

She waved toward the zombies. "Talk to them. Get them to come here?"

He leaned forward. "Because I have been chosen to prepare this part of the world."

Kylie's eyes narrowed. "Prepare this part of the world? For what?"

He sighed, impatiently. "I have been chosen by my Master to prepare the world for the day of his arrival."

"Whose arrival?" asked Allie, her heart hammering in her chest.

He smiled darkly. "Lucifer, child. Who else?"

21

"It looks pretty quiet," said Henry, as they parked outside of Nora's grandmother's house – a small bungalow nestled between two very old willow trees.

Nora opened the passenger door. "It always looked this way."

There were no vehicles parked near the house, which I figured was a fairly bad sign. "Sorry, Nora, I don't think he's here," I said, getting out of the truck.

"Yeah, I know. I don't either," she said, walking toward the front door. "But that doesn't mean he won't show up at one point. I'll leave him another note, tell him that we're going to the Mall of America."

"Just hold up there, toots," said Henry, shuffling toward her with his shotgun. "Let me go in first, in case there are any uninvited guests. I'll introduce them to my double-barrel."

"Henry, we got this," said Nora, walking up the stairway to the porch.

He followed her. "And I've got the gun, now step aside."

Sighing, Nora moved out of the way and Henry put his hand on the doorknob.

"It's locked," he said.

Sighing, Nora stepped off the porch and then went around the back of the house. A few seconds later, she returned, holding a key. "Grams always kept a spare under the birdbath," she said with a sad smile.

"Smart woman," said Henry.

Nora slid the key in and unlocked it. Then she stepped out of the way.

"Just stay behind me," ordered Henry. "And you'll be safe."

They stepped into a small, cluttered living room.

"Your grandma liked fairies?" asked Henry, staring at the two large glass curios containing dozens of small figurines.

"Wow," I said, glancing toward several shelves that contained fairies of every shape, size, and color.

Nora nodded. "That's why she didn't freak out when I got my fairy tattoo. She actually thought it was cool."

"Sounds like your grandma was pretty hip," said Henry.

"She was," said Nora. "It's just a shame that she was frightened of the outside world."

"What do you mean?" asked Henry.

"She had Agoraphobia," said Nora. "She was afraid to go anywhere beyond this house."

"I once knew someone with that phobia," said Henry. "It was weird, though. The woman never mentioned it until I called her for a second date – said it had flared back up and she couldn't leave the house."

I thought he was joking and had to bite back a smile when I noticed he was dead serious.

A noise from somewhere in the back of the house startled us.

"Sounds like a zombie," whispered Henry, when they heard it again – a loud, gurgling moan. "What's back there, Nora?"

"Dammit, that's my bedroom," whispered Nora.

Henry raised his gun. "Stay behind."

We followed Henry down the hallway until we reached Nora's bedroom. He put his hand on the door and took a deep breath.

"Get ready," I whispered to Nora.

He threw open the door and we all gasped in horror.

"Oh, my God," choked Nora as she stared at the gruesome scene. "Daddy!"

Her father, who I knew only from his album covers, was lying on the bed, his lifeless eyes staring up at the ceiling. Standing over him was Nora's grandmother, snacking heartily on his entrails. She turned, and when she noticed us gaping at her, dropped her meal.

"Stand back!" hollered Henry, pointing the rifle.

"No!" hollered Nora, pushing him away.

"Nora, it's not really your grandma anymore!" I yelled as the creature shuffled toward us.

Sobbing, Nora took out her knife and went after the zombie. With a quick jab to her forehead, Nora stabbed the zombie and it fell face-forward onto the ground. "I'm sorry," she whispered, going down onto her knees. She turned her grandmother's still form over, wiped the blood away from her mouth with a blanket that had fallen, and closed her eyelids. "I'll never forget you, Grams," she said, swiping at the fresh tears on her cheeks.

"God, Nora," I said, feeling my own eyes fill up. "I'm so sorry."

She didn't say anything. Instead, she stood up and walked over to her father. "He came back for me," she said, her lips trembling. She reached over and grabbed a blanket, covering his mutilated torso. She then ran a hand over his long, dark hair and smiled bitterly. "I can't believe it."

"He did," said Henry. "See, Nora, your dad loved you."

She nodded and closed her father's eyelids. Then she kissed the top of his head. "I loved you, too, dad," she said.

All three of us stood there in silence for a while, until Nora cleared her throat. "Okay. Enough of this; being a sniveling sap isn't going to help matters. Let's go."

"Okay," I said.

When we got back out to the truck, she stared at the house and her eyes filled with angry tears once again. "My fault, you know. I should have checked the basement."

"What do you mean?" I asked.

She laid her head back on the headrest and closed her eyes. "Before I left for Atlanta. I knew she'd gotten the flu shot – she'd told me that a nurse had come to the house and given it to her earlier in the week. Well, when the zombies started waking up all over town, and I couldn't find Grams at the house, I assumed she'd turned and just walked away in search of food. But, I didn't check the basement."

"You couldn't have known," I said.

She let out a ragged sigh. "But it had bugged me later, after I left the house. I almost went back to check but then I was in too much of a hurry."

"It's not your fault," said Henry. "Don't go blaming yourself for any of this."

"Yeah, but he'd obviously been searching for me when she killed him."

"Of course he was," he said. "Because he loved you, Nora. But don't you, for one second, think that any of this was your fault, including his death. He let his guard down and that's not something any of us can afford to do. Especially when nobody is around to watch our back."

She wiped her cheeks and sat up straighter. "I know, it's just that we were *so* close to finding him. If we wouldn't have wasted so much time at the church, but," her face darkened, "that asshole Travis and his sidekick, Dweeb. As far as I'm concerned, it's their fault that my father died the way he did."

"Well, they did slow us up a bit," said Henry, taking out his can of chew.

She tapped her fingernails on the side of the door and nodded. "Yeah, if I ever see those two evil assholes again, I'm gonna send them where they belong. To Hell."

"Hey, let's hope we don't," I said. That Travis really scared the *hell* out of me.

"But if we do," she said. "I'm going to make sure they pay heavily for threatening the lives of those kids and slowing us down. They'll be begging me for mercy before I'm done with them."

"Oh, Nora," chuckled Henry. "Chances are we'll never see them again."

"Probably not, but there's always hope," she said, closing her eyes.

Funny how the things we hope for can come back to haunt us.

22

"They're back," said Tiny.

Kristie, who'd fallen asleep in a recliner, opened her eyes. "Which ones?" she asked, standing up.

"Paige and Bryce," he said, staring out the window. "Looks like Paige has… oh wow… a baby."

"A *baby*?" gasped Kristie. "What the hell? They weren't even gone that long!"

Tiny chuckled and followed her out of the house.

Kristie stormed over to Paige and pointed at her. "First of all, young lady, I am *so* pissed off with you right now I could just scream."

"Chill out, mom, and look at what we brought you," smiled Paige.

Kristie's face softened as Paige handed her the baby. "Where did you find this little one?" she asked in a softer tone.

"Long story," said Bryce, moving next to Kristie. The baby stared up at him and her lip began to tremble.

"Back away from the baby," said Paige. "You know she doesn't like you."

"She does *so* like me," said Bryce, scowling.

The baby started crying and Bryce stalked away.

"See," said Paige. "You scare her, karate man. Just keep your distance."

"Oh… it's okay, sweetie," cooed Kristie. "Aren't you just the cutest little thing?"

The baby stopped crying and smiled up at Kristie, whose heart immediately melted.

"So, can we keep her?" asked Paige.

"Well, babies are a lot of work, honey," said Kristie. "And they need a lot of attention. I just don't know..."

Bryce rubbed a hand over his face. "Hello! It's not like we can just drop her off anywhere. Obviously, we're going to have to keep her."

"You *are* crabby, aren't you?" chuckled Kristie.

"You would be too if you had to risk your life getting diapers and formula. I didn't expect to do that this soon in life. It's very... sobering."

"Hey, where's Billie?" asked Tiny.

"He must have fallen asleep again," said Bryce. "He was bitten by a zombie."

"What!" snapped Kristie.

Bryce went over the events as they unfolded, starting with finding Paige in the SUV.

"You think he's going to change into a zombie?" asked Tiny.

"I really don't know," said Bryce. "He was feverish and in a lot of pain. Fortunately, he didn't lose as much blood as I originally thought."

"What should we do?" asked Kristie, staring toward the SUV.

"I don't know. I have enough things to worry about. This is your call," said Bryce.

"Just keep a close eye on him," said Tiny. "We'll take turns watching him. After what happened to that crazy broad, Eva, I'm not taking any chances."

"And don't forget about Austin," said Paige. "He blew up your gas station."

He sighed. "That's right. We can't afford to take our eyes off of him. You guys with me?'

"Definitely," said Bryce. "In fact, I'll take the first shift."

"Let's get him into the house," said Tiny.

"You're grounded, by the way," said Kristie, placing the baby on her shoulder and bouncing her gently.

Paige frowned. "You can't ground me, mother."

"The hell I can't."

"I'm eighteen."

"Then act your age and quit adding more trouble to our situation. You put yourself, as well as these guys, in more danger when you snuck off like that."

"If it wasn't for me, Billie might have died and the baby as well!"

"Paige –"

"No!" hollered Paige. "Quit treating me like I'm some kind of princess! I'm a grown woman, with opinions, a temper, and a hell of a right hook."

"Yes, I know," said Kristie, "but –"

"No buts, mother. Look at me! I'm not a little girl anymore. In fact, what I am is… a soldier, one who's killed more people in the last few weeks than a freaken' serial killer would in a lifetime, and I don't know about you, but I'm handling it pretty damn well."

"Yes, honey, I know. I just don't want anything happening to you. I'd never forgive myself."

"Nothing will. Look, I wasn't born yesterday and I'm not going to put myself in a situation I know I can't handle. You just have to have a little more faith in me, mom. Seriously."

Kristie sighed. "Fine, but no more lying or sneaking around."

"And no more sheltering me from the world," said Paige. "Not only is it annoying, but it's degrading."

"I'll try, really I will. I just don't want to lose you."

"You won't," she said, softening her voice.

Kristie stared at her intently and then sighed. "Fine. You're growing up and there's nothing I can do to stop it. Look, I'll ease up on you and even give you a little more space."

"I guess that's all I can ask," she said, walking back toward the house.

Kristie shook her head and looked at Tiny. "You know, when I was a teenager, all my mother had to worry about was me sneaking off to go to a party or getting knocked up by one of my dates. Hell, that's nothing compared to this shit. I have to worry about my daughters sneaking off like freedom fighters in the middle of the night, and whether or not they took the right weapon to bludgeon a damn zombie to death. And now," she said, looking down at the baby in her arms. "Another little princess has been delivered to my doorstep. I don't know whether to laugh or cry."

"Sounds like someone above thinks you're a pretty good mother," said Tiny, putting an arm around her.

"Or he's making me pay for all the hell I raised when I was a kid. Is that it, honey?" she asked the baby, who was stared up at her. "Is this my penance for all the trouble I gave my own mother?"

The baby grinned.

***

"Let me guess," said Billie, who was lying down in the guestroom of the house, "you're my babysitter."

Bryce sat down on the floor and leaned his head against the wall. "We just want to keep an eye on you, bro. Just in case."

"Just in case," smirked Billie. "Well, it's kind of unnerving, you know. Everyone keeps looking at me like they don't know me. Like I'm going to turn on them and rip their throat out."

He opened up a bottle of water and took a sip. "You're overdramatizing everything. They're a little worried, but they still care about you, man. Just chill out."

Billie closed his eyes. "This is a nightmare. I just can't believe one of those things got to me."

"Yeah, it was a bad scene. I'm sorry I took so long on the boat."

"It wasn't your fault," he said, opening his eyes back up. "I slipped and fell. End of story."

"But still…"

"Look, Paige was right there and she couldn't stop it from happening either. The zombie was fast, man."

Bryce took another sip of his water and noticed the sweat on Billie's forehead. "You okay? You want something to drink?"

"Actually, yeah. I'm parched. I think I need some more aspirin, too. My fever must be coming back in full force."

Bryce stood up. "Okay," he said. "Don't go anywhere."

Billie closed his eyes. "I'm not planning on it."

Bryce left the room and walked to the kitchen, where he found Tiny staring out the window. "What's up?"

"I don't want to go freaking anyone out," he whispered. "But I think someone's out there. And I'm not just talking zombies."

Bryce moved to the window and looked out into the backyard. "What did you see?"

"I saw movement. By the shed."

Both men stood staring out the window, when they heard Kristie scream.

Tiny bolted out of the kitchen and down the hallway to the living room.

"Tiny, oh my God, he took the baby!" cried Kristie, who was alone by the front door.

"Who?" asked Bryce.

"Billie! I was rocking her in the chair when he rushed out of the bedroom, snatched her out of my arms, and then took off running outside."

Bryce ran out the door and toward the dark street. Hearing the baby's cries, he turned toward the sound and in the distance he could see Billie's silhouette.

"Billie!" he hollered, racing toward him.

Billie ignored him and kept running.

"What the hell, Billie?!" he yelled again, the distance between them getting shorter. "Stop!"

Just then, a vehicle turned the corner and headlights lit up the road. Billie stopped running and turned back to face Bryce.

"What are you doing, man?" asked Bryce, stopping a few feet away.

Billie's eyes were bloodshot and his skin was almost a grayish color. "Have to bring him the baby. Have to bring him the baby. Have to…"

"Whoa," said Bryce, holding up his hands. "Just calm down."

The vehicle, a Honda Odyssey, stopped and the doors flew open.

"Bryce!" yelled Cassie, rushing toward him.

"Thank God," sighed Bryce, as she threw herself in his arms. He closed his eyes and released a ragged sigh.

"Billie?" smiled Nora.

"Wait! Don't go near him!" yelled Bryce, opening his eyes. He turned to her and held out a hand. "Nora, please, don't get near him, he's been bitten and is starting to act crazy."

Nora's face fell. "What?"

Henry slammed the door of the truck and slowly walked toward them. "What's that?"

Nora took a step forward. "Billie?"

"What are you doing with that baby, Billie?" asked Henry, spitting out a wad of chew.

Billie stared at them, his eyes wild and his face covered in perspiration. "I'm… I have to take her to him… all the babies have to be found and taken to him."

"Who's him?" asked Henry.

Billie opened his mouth, but instead of answering, began running with the baby again.

"Billie!" hollered Nora, taking off after him.

Bryce and Cassie quickly followed suit.

***

Billie ran, clutching the baby tighter. He didn't exactly understand why he felt such an overwhelming urge take her south, or who "he" was, but the desperation seemed to consume him.

"Stop, Billie!" yelled Nora.

Nora.

His muddled mind cleared slightly and his heart began to swell. He stopped and then turned to find himself looking down into her eyes.

God, he'd missed her.

"Give me the baby," she demanded, holding out her arms.

"No, I can't. I have to do this."

Swearing under her breath, she reached out and tried to grab the baby herself.

"No!" he growled, backhanding her.

She fell to the ground and then quickly got back up. "You asshole," she snarled, "nobody hits me! I don't care how many times we've made out!"

"I... I'm sorry," he said, horrified of what he'd just done.

Bring the child, demanded the voice in his head.

He turned to run, again, when someone grabbed his arm, yanking him backwards.

"Thank you," said Cassie, snatching the baby from his arms while Bryce subdued him with a strangle-hold.

"Let me go," he pleaded, his voice hoarse. "I have to bring the baby to him."

"Bullshit," snarled Nora, storming toward him. "Let him go, Bryce."

Bryce released him and the last thing he remembered before the darkness came, was Nora's foot slamming into his chin.

23

"Don't you *ever* leave me again," he whispered into my hair.

"Bryce," I said, "I can't breathe."

He loosened his arms around my waist and sighed. "What were you thinking? Seriously, what were you thinking?"

I stepped back, avoiding his eyes. "Don't start with me."

"They're in Atlanta, you know. Your grandparents. If you wouldn't have taken off the way you did, you'd probably be reunited as we speak."

"Atlanta is a big city, Bryce. Chances are we wouldn't have passed each other on the streets."

"Your sister is still out there."

My heart stopped.

My sister?

I looked up at him in horror. "What?"

"Guess you two have more in common than you thought. She left with Kylie and Luke, to search for you."

"When?" I asked.

"Right after you left."

"Oh, my God," I moaned, closing my eyes. "It's too dangerous for those girls to be out on the road."

He nodded. "Exactly. Too dangerous for all of you. My only consolation was that you had Henry backing you up. Luke, though, Luke is just a kid."

"We have to find them," I said, storming out of the bedroom.

I had to find *her*.

My little sister.

He followed me. "Yeah, well we've been trying to do that without any luck. I think we should stick around here, see if they show up, like you guys just did. I think our odds are better there."

I began to pace. "I just found her and now she's missing again? And now Kylie, too! Oh, my God, what were they thinking?"

"What were *they* thinking? Isn't it obvious?"

I stopped. "What, that she feels like I abandoned her?"

"Those are your words, not mine. Obviously, she loves you and wants to be with you."

Sitting down in the armchair, I put my head in my hands. "I don't know what to do now."

"Like I said, we wait here for a few days and see if she shows up."

I nodded and stood up. "Okay. Meanwhile, I'm going to the Mall of America."

His eyes widened. "Excuse me? Now isn't the time to shop for a new purse."

I told him about the man on the radio and how they were urging other survivors to join them. "Maybe the girls heard him, too, and decided to go there first?"

"Maybe. Well, obviously I'm coming with you," he said.

Just then, Paige walked into the living room. "Okay, where are you going now?"

I told her what we'd heard on the radio and she immediately volunteered to join us.

"You should stay here," said Bryce.

She glared at him. "Don't tell me what to do. Kylie is my sister and I'm leaving here with you guys."

"She should come," I said. Paige had already gone off on me about leaving her behind in Atlanta and I wasn't about to piss her off again. Besides, it was her sister that was missing, just like mine.

Bryce sighed. "Fine."

"Well, Billie is still unconscious," said Kristie, walking into the room. "We have him tied up and Nora is watching him."

"What in the hell was he doing with Adria?" asked Paige. "Is he going crazy or something?"

Bryce shrugged. "I don't know. He's been acting strange ever since that zombie bit him."

"A zombie bit him? How long ago?" I asked.

"About four hours," answered Bryce.

I closed my eyes and sighed.

Poor Billie.

My fault.

"Nora is pretty distraught," said Kristie. "First, seeing her father, and now Billie. I think she really cares about him."

"Has he been showing signs of aggression or other disturbing behavior?" I asked, opening my eyes.

"Stealing a baby and running off into the night, that's pretty disturbing," said Bryce. "He was also mumbling something about taking the baby to 'him.' We just can't trust Billie anymore."

"He might pull through this," I said. "Allie and I did."

"Maybe. But for now we're going to have to watch him closely and keep him away from the baby," said Kristie. "Where's Henry and Adria?"

"I think they're outside on the porch," I said. "Watching the sunrise together."

Kristie smiled. "Did you see the way his eyes lit up when Adria smiled at him?"

"He loves children," I said, and then told her about our ordeal at the church.

Paige scowled. "What kind of a person would try to torch a church?"

"And one filled with children," I added. "God, I hope Allie and Kylie don't run into these guys. The chances are slim, but…"

"Which way were these two knuckleheads traveling?" asked Kristie.

"I have no idea," I said.

"Well, let's get going," said Bryce. "We shouldn't waste any more time."

Kristie's eyebrows shot up. "Where in the hell are you going now?"

I filled her in on the radio transmission.

"You think Allie and Kylie might have gone out there to meet that guy?"

"I don't know, but it's worth checking out. For all we know, the girls beat us to Minnesota, heard the announcement, and decided to see what was happening there. You know those two and malls." I smiled. "An open mall with designer clothing and millions of shoes at their disposal. It'd be like winning the lottery for them."

She smirked. "Now *I'm* starting to get jealous! Well, we'll hang out here and see if they show up while you go to Bloomington. Who knows, you might even find your grandparents there."

"They're supposed to be in Atlanta," I said.

"Are you kidding me? *Nobody* is where they're supposed to be," said Kristie.

"This is true," I said.

"I'm going with them," informed Paige.

Kristie nodded reluctantly. "Fine, but listen to Bryce and don't try any more crazy heroics."

"Okay," said Paige as Kristie kissed the top of her head.

"I'm going to tell Henry," I said, walking out the front.

"Tell me what?" he asked, as I shut the door and joined him on the porch. Adria was in his arms and he was in my grandfather's favorite rocking chair, rocking her gently.

"We're going to MOA."

He snorted. "Leave it to teenaged girls and shopping – not even a zombie apocalypse will stand in the way."

"Well, you heard that guy – there should be other survivors out that way. More people we might know. *Maybe* even Allie and Kylie."

"Maybe," he said. "Well, obviously I'm coming with you, too."

"No, you should stay here," I said. "Get some rest."

"Oh, I've got all eternity to rest," he said, holding the baby out to me. "Here, now take little Adria, so I can go drop some kids off to the pool before we set sail."

I looked down at the sleeping baby and felt an odd sense of peace. Here we were, in the middle of an apocalypse, my sister and Kylie were missing, Billie had been bitten by a zombie, and we'd witnessed Nora's father getting murdered by her zombie grandmother. But amazingly, for the first time in weeks, I felt a wave of hope wash over me. Even with all of the obstacles we still faced, something told me that things were going to be okay.

Her eyelids fluttered open and she stared at me.

"Don't worry, Adria," I whispered. "Things are going to be okay. I won't let anything happen to you."

Her little bowtie lips curled up into a smile and something told me that she believed it.

24

"Hey," said Bryce, grabbing my hand. "We need to talk."

"I thought we already did," I said, following him into the bedroom. He'd taken a shower and was wearing a new pair of Levis and a white T-shirt that hugged his still very-chiseled pecs. I had to admit, even though he'd lost a little weight and had dark circles under his eyes, he still made my pulse race with that sexy little smile of his.

He closed the door and then turned to me. "We have talked, several times, but you never seem to really listen to what I have to say. So I've decided to try another approach."

Before I could respond, he grabbed me around the waist and pulled me into his arms.

"What are you doing?" I asked, feeling my cheeks turn pink. "I don't think we have time…"

"We don't," he whispered, staring into my eyes. "And that's why we have to make every minute count." Then his lips found mine and I soon found myself underneath him on the bed.

"I've missed you so much," he said, pulling my shirt over my head.

"Me too," I answered, gasping as his hands began moving around my body.

Four minutes and twenty-three seconds later, he was gasping above me and I was staring up at him in   amusement.

He turned onto his side and touched my lips with his fingertips. "You're so beautiful."

"Thank you."

"Sorry," he said, smiling sheepishly. "I know that was too fast, but I just lost control."

"No, it was fantastic," I said. "Short and sweet. Kind of like those miniature candy bars, where they're so awesome that you just can't eat one, but if you only have one, it leaves you still craving more."

He stared at me for a second and then burst out laughing. "Is that supposed to make me feel better?"

"I'm just saying… I wasn't… dissatisfied, I'm just still… craving you," I said, kissing his lips.

"I don't know what's more disturbing, comparing me to a miniature candy bar, or reminding me that it just wasn't enough to settle your craving. Both could be construed as rips on my manhood."

I stood up and slipped my shorts back on. "Are you kidding me? Your manhood is… just… awesome. I mean, it's the best out there, I'm sure."

"Because you've had so much experience, you'd know?" he said, his eyes sparkling.

"I know that I'm more than happy, and that's all that matters."

Someone began pounding on the bedroom door. "Hey, you two done talking about candy in there?" hollered Henry. "Because we're all waiting for you so we can leave."

My face turned bright red.

"Don't worry," whispered Bryce, kissing me, again, "he doesn't know what we were up to."

I bit the side of my lip. "Okay."

After we left the bedroom, I overheard Henry teasing Bryce about adding a little more nuts to his candy bars, and I had to leave the room so he wouldn't see me laughing.

***

"Everyone set?" asked Bryce, starting the van. "You all have weapons and water?"

"Yeah," I said, buckling my seatbelt. Paige and I both had metal bats, Henry had his double-barrel shotgun, and Bryce had found a hunting knife along with one of my grandfather's guns, a three-fifty-seven Magnum, in the basement. I couldn't believe he'd left it.

"Take this, too," said Bryce, tossing me a pocket knife. "I feel better knowing that you have a backup if you lose the bat."

"What about me?" asked Paige, who was sitting next to me in the second row.

"Well, you're all set, girl. You've got that bat and a sharp tongue. The zombies don't have a chance."

She slapped his shoulder. "Not funny."

"I wasn't joking," he said, and then flinched when she raised her fist to club him.

"Now, let Bryce drive, Paige," said Henry. "You can beat the tar out of him later. Kick him in the Snickers."

Page snorted. "Snickers?"

"Well from what I understand, they certainly aren't Almond Joys," chuckled Henry.

"Okay, enough," said Bryce. "You don't know what the hell you're talking about."

"That's right," I said. "Besides, we need to focus on finding the girls and not Bryce's goodies."

Paige wrinkled her nose. "Uh, I agree. Unless you want me to hurl, don't mention sex and Bryce in the same sentence."

Trying not to laugh, I changed the subject. "I hope they can handle Billie if he becomes a zombie," I said, remembering how volatile Eva and Austin had become when they'd both went through their changes.

"I think Nora can handle him, along with a dozen other zombies, *at* the same time, *with* her eyes closed," said Paige.

I stared out the window and smiled. "Yeah, she's one person I'm glad to have on our side, that's for sure."

The rain started and everyone became silent. Bryce turned on the wipers as we turned onto the highway.

"Looks like this one is going to be another doozy," remarked Henry, staring up at the dark clouds. "Mother Nature's been pretty moody these last few days. So unpredictable."

"It's been like that for a while," I said. "Nobody's noticed it as much because we're all focused on staying alive."

"True," said Henry, lowering his hat over his eyes. "At least we don't have to worry about earthquakes in Minnesota. That last one in Atlanta was a little unnerving."

Bryce snorted. "You spoke too soon, Henry. There was one yesterday."

I leaned forward. "What? An earthquake in Minnesota? Seriously?"

Paige nodded. "Yeah, we had a couple of them yesterday. Nothing major, but you could tell it was a quake."

"That is so weird," I said.

"Billie and Tiny think it's the end of the world," said Paige.

"Huh. Well, it's not the first time we've heard that statement in the last few days," I said. "Is it, Henry?"

"Nope."

"The nuns we met the other day also claimed the same thing. Said it was the 'End of Days'."

"Okay, please clarify exactly what that means. End of everything, shorter days, what?" asked Paige.

"Well," I said, "if you've ever read the Bible –"

"No, can't say that I have," she replied, smiling sheepishly. "But I've watched the History Channel quite a bit. There's more stuff on there about our rocky future than what happened yesterday."

"I know. So, um, what did the nun say, again, Henry?"

He cleared his throat. "Oh, she mentioned the seven signs of the apocalypse."

"What are they?" asked Paige.

He sighed. "Deadly plagues, hunger, and earthquakes. Then the sky will turn dark, and the water will turn to blood. Finally, Satan will emerge to fight the final battle between good and evil."

"Billie said the same thing," replied Paige.

"Well, at least the water hasn't changed color," I laughed. "Then I'd be a little more paranoid."

Paige looked at me. "Seriously, did you *not* notice the lake by your grandparents' house?"

"Uh, I guess not."

"Bryce, tell them."

"The lake wasn't red, Paige, it was pink," he replied.

"See, there you go," said Paige.

"Like I said before, there could be a number of reasons," said Bryce. "We already went over this."

"Yeah, well what about the river?" said Paige.

He shrugged. "Same thing."

I raised my eyebrows. "The river was red?"

"It was just pink," said Bryce. "And it smelled awful so I'm sure it was contaminated. Somehow."

Paige groaned. "God, that man of yours is so close-minded."

His jaw clenched. "It's not the end of the world and I'm not jumping on that bandwagon. The world is going to Hell, but it's because of us and what *we've* done to it. Nothing spiritual or based on religion. I mean, come on."

"Do you believe in God?" she asked.

I held my breath. I hadn't even asked Bryce, and now that we were engaged, I was a little unnerved of what his answer was.

"To tell you the truth, I don't really know. Obviously, I want to believe that there is something else out there and not just us."

"Are you talking aliens or God?" smirked Paige.

Bryce sighed. "Okay, let me rephrase my statement – I *hope* that there is a God. I hope that all of these people who were killed, the ones who became zombies, are not just... lost forever."

"What about you, Henry?" asked Paige.

Henry didn't answer, he was too busy snoring.

"Cassie?" she asked me.

"You know how I feel," I said to her.

"Not really. It's not like we sit around talking about religion and what shade of lip gloss looks the best under the chapel lights."

I smiled. "You goof."

She stared at me. "Seriously, tell us."

I pulled my hair to the side. "I'm a Christian, what more can I say? What about you?"

She sighed. "Me too, and that's why I'm scared to death of what may or may not be happening."

"Paige, any one of us could die at any moment. I mean, who knows, we could be walking into some kind of trap at MOA," I said. "Hell, after getting kidnapped more than once these last few weeks, I'm not discounting anything."

"In other words, this could be another suicide mission?" she asked, a horrified look on her face.

I sighed. "I'm just saying that you shouldn't dwell on something that may or may not happen. Live for now and quit worrying about 'signs' and bloody rivers and lakes."

"You're seriously not freaked out about any of this?" she asked.

I shook my head. "No, what I'm worried about, more than anything, is finding our sisters. *Alive.*"

Henry stretched his arms and yawned. "What you all should be worried about is finding me a hopper. I don't know what I ate, but you kids are going to *wish* for merciful death if we don't do something about it real soon."

Bryce swore under his breath. "I thought you went to the bathroom before we left the house?"

"I did, but that doesn't mean I got it all out. Sometimes things get stuck on the edge and don't slip out until later."

I shuddered. "Okay, T.M.I., Henry. Bryce, just find a place for him to go."

Henry began rolling down his window. "Oh, false alarm. Just a little gas. Pardon me, ladies."

We all rolled the windows down.

"You should have brought the Vicks," chuckled Bryce, waving his hand.

"Henry's gas has found a way past even the heaviest of mentholated vapo-rub," I said. "Believe me, it doesn't help with him. Ask Nora."

"What can I say? When you get to be my age, sometimes things fester and you never know what's going to pass through those bottom gates."

"God, enough of the fart talk," said Bryce, turning on the radio. "Which radio station was that guy on in Bloomington?"

Henry reached forward and started turning the stations until he finally reached one that actually had a song playing, an old one by the Beatles called "Let It Be."

"What do you know?" smiled Henry, turning it up. "Now those boys knew how to shake things up, including the ladies. Why, I remember this woman I dated in England, she was crazy about Paul McCartney and would do these little strip-teases for me when I would put on any of their old records."

"First of all," I interrupted. "You lived in England for a while? You never mentioned that."

He waved his hand. "Oh, just a couple of years. Anyway, that girl had these little tassels," he said, raising his fingers to his chest, "and boy she could get those things shaking and twirling, by golly. It was quite the show, let me tell you."

"Wonder if they have any of those kind of tassels at the mall?" joked Bryce, looking back at me.

"Keep your eyes on the road," I said, my face flushed.

Paige groaned. "Guys, just listen to the song."

Everyone became silent as the song went on and when it was finished, the same voice from the other day began speaking once again.

"Whether you're just tuning in or you've been listening to us and are still trying to figure things out, we are *here* for you. You don't have to do this alone, not anymore. Point your truck, your car, hell, your motorcycle and come join us. Let me tell you, brothers and sisters, every day, more survivors are appearing at our doorstep, lost and nearly giving up hope on everything. But you don't have to give up *anything*. I'm telling you, all you have to do is join us and you won't have to worry about food, water, or whether or not you're going to survive another restless night with these walking dead. We're all in the same boat. We've all lost loved ones – our spouses, our children, our friends, and neighbors. We've all been to Hell and back, but no more! No more, I tell you! Here, there is hope, there is support, and there is a place waiting for you…"

"What is he, some kind of preacher or something?" asked Paige.

"I don't know. He sounds like a decent enough person, though," I replied. "Like he just wants to help us all."

"Don't judge anyone by words," said Henry. "This guy might not be what he seems."

"What do you mean?" asked Paige.

Henry turned to look back at me. "Come on, Wild. Listen to his voice."

His voice had sounded vaguely familiar but it wasn't until Henry had pointed it out, too, that it all came back to me.

I stared at him in horror. "Travis."

Henry nodded gravely.

25

"Did you hear that?" asked Kylie, staring through the metal gates toward the faint cries down the hallway. Two hours earlier, they'd been forced into one of the smaller clothing stores in the mall, locked inside without food or water.

"It sounds like they've found another baby," whispered Allie. "I think this is the third one we've heard."

Kylie turned to her. "Where are these babies coming from? And why are they here?"

Allie, who was sitting on the ground, pulled her legs in closer to her chest. "I have no idea," she answered. "And I don't think I want to know."

"I hope he's not hurting them."

"Let's hope."

Kylie sighed. "We have to get out of here and try to help them."

"The babies? How? We're locked in. Even if we were to somehow find a way out, the mall is surrounded by zombies. Face it, Kylie," she said, her eyes filling with tears, "we are *never* getting out of here alive, especially with those babies. We're all doomed."

"Don't say that."

Allie wiped a tear from her cheek. "But, it's true. This guy isn't human. You saw his red eyes. And, what if what he says is true?" she lowered her voice. "What if Satan is coming?"

Kylie bit the side of her lip. "Yeah, but 'good' is always supposed to conquer 'evil'. We've been reading about that our entire lives."

"Sure, but that's mostly in storybooks, Kylie. This is real. At least, I think it is. I don't know about you, but I haven't seen anything good for a very long time."

Kylie kneeled next to her. "Don't say that! You survived a zombie bite, so did your sister. You're still alive, Allie. Don't give up hope."

"Tell that to my parents, or to Luke, or to the mothers of those babies those guys are stealing! How can we have hope when we've been imprisoned by somebody who might actually be an honest to goodness demon? I mean, even if there was a chance for us, nobody knows where we are."

"But, there's always Justice," said Kylie. "He might be able to help us still."

"Justice?" she scoffed. "He's not with us anymore. I mean, seriously, he doesn't even know his own name. Obviously, that demon did something to him."

"I still think there's hope. Maybe if we can get him alone, we can talk to him," said Kylie, standing up. "Help him snap out of it."

"Maybe."

Another noise from somewhere in the mall, this time a woman's harrowing cries, echoed through the darkness and the girls became silent. Kylie sat down next to Allie and they held hands.

***

Justice watched as more zombies, and this time living, breathing people, arrived at the mall. After getting instructions from Travis, they all took off in different directions, prepared to do whatever task he had assigned them.

Very bad things were about to happen, he thought. *And much worse than anything seen in the last few weeks.*

Although he understood and was horrified, he was physically unable to do anything about it. His limbs wouldn't follow any of the simplest instructions, nor could he communicate on his own any longer. He felt like a puppet, one that was being manipulated by one very evil puppet master.

"Dwayne," said Travis, after dismissing another small group of zombies. "What is happening with the infants?"

"Still no luck."

Travis's face darkened. "He has to be here somewhere. The signs all point to this region."

"We'll find the child," said Dwayne. "If he is here, we'll find him eventually."

"We don't have 'eventually'," snarled Travis. "It has to be soon. Very soon."

Dwayne nodded. "Yes, sir."

Travis suddenly closed his eyes and stood still for several minutes, almost as if he'd fallen asleep. Eventually, he opened his eyes and nodded. "Excellent."

"What?" asked Dwayne.

"I have been given great news," said Travis. He turned toward Justice and his face broke out into a chilling grin. "Justice, it is time that we check on your friends."

Justice felt nauseous. *Why is he doing this?*

"Why? Well, there is a reason as to why our paths have crossed, Justice. It was destiny."

Justice, who had been standing in one place for several hours, found himself moving toward Travis without his control.

"Follow Dwayne. Get those sweet, young girlfriends of yours and bring them to me." He turned to Dwayne. "Now you will see exactly why we needed them alive."

"I never doubted you," said Dwayne.

"Go."

Justice followed Dwayne back into Nordstrom's and into a darker section of the mall.

"Justice!" squealed Kylie, standing up behind the metal enclosure. "Oh, thank God you're here!"

He tried opening his mouth to respond, but found he couldn't.

"Stand back," demanded Dwayne, searching through a large set of keys.

The girls obeyed, and soon they were released from the gate enclosure.

"We've missed you," cried Kylie, throwing her arms around him. When he made no attempt to return the hug, she stepped backwards and stared up at him. "Justice?"

Staring at the two confused and frightened girls, he tried to speak, to tell them he was going to get them the hell out of there, but he still couldn't move his lips or tongue.

"I see you," said Kylie, searching his eyes with hers. "I'm not sure what's wrong with you, if you've been drugged or possessed by some kind of evil spirit, but I still see *you*."

"Let's go," said Dwayne, pointing his gun at the girls. "Move."

Possessed? Was something really possessing his body? The thought was horrifying, but something told him that it really wasn't too far from the truth. He had no control of his body, although he knew what was right and wrong, could still think and feel every emotion.

They started back toward Nordstrom's with Dwayne following behind, trying to light a cigarette. Justice could hear the girls whispering frantically behind him.

"Justice," murmured Kylie, clutching his arm. "You have to try and overcome this, whatever it is. Travis is evil, but you aren't. Please, Justice, if you don't snap out of this, I have a feeling we're all going to die."

Justice tried to respond, but as before, he was still unable to speak.

Allie moved to the other side of him. "Justice, help us. Please," she begged. "For God's sake, you said you didn't believe in God before, but I think he may be our only hope." She removed the cross necklace from around her neck and pressed it into the palm of his hand. She closed it. "This was my mother's. Look, you have to believe and pray, Justice, pray for some kind of a miracle."

"Listen to her. Travis said he is paving the way for Lucifer, Justice. Do you know who that is?" whispered Kylie. "If there is a Devil, then obviously, there is a God."

"That's enough," growled Dwayne, pulling the girls away from Justice. "Quit groping the boy or I'll have to cut you both. Believe me, it will be a great pleasure."

Justice could feel the cross in his palm and thought about what Kylie and Allie had said. It was obvious that whatever was happening to his body wasn't something that could be explained. Still, it was hard to conceive that if there truly was a God, he would allow so much horror, grief, and misery on Earth.

"Oh good," smiled Travis, as the girls were ushered back outside into the early morning light. "They're back."

Justice stared at the large group of people who must have arrived when they'd left to get the girls. These people were dressed in red robes and each had downward-pointed pentagrams painted on their forehead.

Satan worshipers?

They stared at Travis as if he was some kind of god himself, and he felt like retching.

Were they going to sacrifice the girls?

Justice looked at Kylie, who was silently pleading with her eyes for him to do something.

To save them.

Travis grabbed the arms of both Kylie and Allie, pulling them toward the crowd of onlookers. "Our newest disciples!" he hollered, a purely evil smile on his face.

"What? No!" cried Kylie, looking horrified. She tried pulling away from Travis, but he held her firm.

"Oh, my God!" sobbed Allie, staring at the delighted group of people. "Are these *Satanists*?"

"How lovely. Are we going to sacrifice them?" hollered a woman from the crowd with jet-black hair and a wicked smile.

"No, they are going to help us search for the 'chosen one'," he said with a sneer. "Our father says they will lead us to the child."

"Lucifer?" gasped a man, with awe. "Has he arrived?"

"Not yet," said Travis. "It's not yet time for him to grace us with his glory. Right now, we must continue our search for the child and destroy it, before the day of reckoning."

Realizing now why the babies had been brought in, Allie and Kylie stared at each other in horror.

"Please," cried Kylie. "Let us go! We can't lead you anywhere. We don't know of any babies! Most of them have died because of the flu and the zombies."

"Oh, I plan on letting you go," laughed Travis, releasing her hand. "I'll even bring you home to your families." He leaned forward until he was staring into her eyes. "Both of you."

26

"How is he doing?" asked Kristie, stepping into the guestroom.

Nora sighed. "The same."

"Has he woken up at all?"

"No."

"Okay. Well, if you get hungry or thirsty, let me know. I'll bring you something."

"Thanks. So, where did you find that baby?" she asked.

"Bryce, Paige, and Billie found her in Stillwater, when they were trying to search for Cassie's grandparents."

"Oh."

Kristie looked at Billie, who was snoring on the bed. "I still wonder... what in the hell was he going to do with Adria?"

She stretched her legs and yawned. "I think he was just delirious from the virus."

"Yeah, you're probably right."

Nora closed her eyes and opened them again.

Kristie frowned. "Do you need a break? You look tired, hon."

She stood up. "No, I'm fine."

"Okay, well, let me know if you change your mind," said Kristie.

"Thanks."

Kristie nodded and left the room.

Nora sat back down and stared longingly at Billie. Although she wanted nothing more than to lie down next to his body, put her arms around him, and try to somehow comfort him, she knew it was too dangerous.

"Come back to me, Billie," she whispered, blinking back tears. "Please."

***

"My, you were hungry," said Kristie, burping Adria after she'd sucked down an entire bottle of formula. "I guess that's a good thing."

Tiny sat next to her on the couch and smiled. "You're a good mother, Kristie."

"Mother? I'm going to be old enough to be a grandmother in another ten years."

"Ten years, huh?" he said, his eyes twinkling.

"Damn straight. My girls are not having kids until they're close to thirty."

"Well, since there are not many single men left on this planet, those are some pretty good odds."

"Here," said Kristie. "Hold her for a minute, will you?"

"Uh, she's kind of small. What if I hurt her?"

"Relax, you're not going to hurt her," she said, placing Adria into his muscular arms.

Tiny looked down at the baby, who gave him a wide, toothless grin. "She sure is a sweet little thing," he said as she grasped his index finger.

"You two have a lot in common," said Kristie, standing up. "You're *both* sweet and bald."

"Just don't tell everyone," whispered Tiny as Kristie left the room. "Wrestler-slash-zombie-killers are definitely not supposed to be sweet. Show no mercy is our motto, you know?"

The baby giggled and Tiny felt as if his heart had outgrown his massive chest.

***

"Nora," whispered Billie hoarsely.

Nora opened her eyes.

Crap, she'd fallen asleep.

"How do you feel?" she asked, moving closer to the bed.

He sat up and released a ragged breath. "Like shit."

She reached over and touched his forehead. "You're burning up. I'll get you some aspirin."

"My wrists hurt," he said. "Can you please untie me?"

Her eyes narrowed. "No."

"Nora, it's me. Come on, babe. Just untie my arms. You can leave my ankles tied up if you want."

"But..."

"Look at my wrists," he said, holding them up. They were indeed red. "The rope is practically cutting off my circulation."

She sighed. "Fine, but you'd better behave."

"Thanks," he said. "I knew you still cared."

She smirked. "You're lucky I didn't beat the crap out of you earlier."

He smiled. "I'm sorry. I guess I'm not quite myself these days. If you'd still like to beat me, I won't resist. It might be kind of fun, actually."

"Oh, yeah?" she laughed, untying him. "You say that now but you have no idea what kind of punishment we're talking about."

He grabbed her wrist and pulled her into his arms. "God, I've missed you," he whispered, searching her face. "So much, in fact, that I've been dreaming about you."

She swallowed. "Um, I've missed you, too."

He slid his hands over her hips and closed his eyes. "You smell so good."

"I do?"

As far as she was concerned, she needed a toothbrush and a hot shower.

He opened his eyes again and she stared in shock at all of the freshly broken capillaries.

"Are you okay?" she asked, stiffening up.

"I'm fine," he said. "Relax." Then, he raised his hand behind her head and pulled her face to his. When his lips touched hers, he made a strange noise in the back of his throat.

"Billie," she murmured, trying to pull away. "Let me get you something. Even your lips are hot." Although she yearned for his kisses, she had to remember, he was obviously infected.

"Please," he pleaded, touching her cheek. "Just let me kiss you. You taste so good and it's been so long."

His words warmed her heart, making her feel more wanted than she had in a very long time. She longed for Billie to hold her, to tell her that everything was going to be all right. Like he had in Atlanta.

Screw it.

"Okay, Billie. But just on the lips, though; no tongue and no saliva."

Smiling, he pulled her back into his arms and found her lips once again. When his tongue slid inside of her mouth, she panicked and tried breaking free from his firm hold.

"No," she gasped, trying to push away from his chest. "It's too dangerous!"

"Smells so good," he growled, crushing his lips to hers once again. He pushed her down on the bed and forced his tongue into her mouth. Before she knew what was happening, he bit her tongue, drawing blood.

"Stop!" she screamed, kicking at him.

Kristie stormed through the door. "What in the hell is going on in here?!"

Billie backed away and Nora jumped off the bed, her face covered with tears.

"I'm sorry!" cried Billie, his face crumbling. "I didn't mean to do that, to hurt you! I... I couldn't help myself."

Nora picked up the ax she'd left on the floor. "You bit my tongue!"

"Nora," what are you doing with that ax?" he asked, staring at her in horror.

"Billie, I'm not going to hurt you. Unless you attack me like that again!"

He held out his hand. "I swear to you, I didn't do it on purpose. I just... I couldn't stop myself."

"It's the zombie virus," said Kristie. "He's already craving flesh."

"No!" gasped Billie. "Hell no!"

"It's true. First the erratic behavior, and now this," said Kristie. "Good thing he didn't get away with Adria."

Billie's eyebrows shot up. "With Adria?"

"Yeah, you tried to kidnap her, don't you remember?" asked Nora.

He looked confused. "No, I... I remember seeing your face and then blacking out. Who is Adria?"

"The baby you found," said Kristie. "In Stillwater."

He slumped back against the pillows and put his head in his hands. "I just can't remember any of what you're telling me."

Kristie turned to Nora. "We have to tie him back up and then I'm going to have Tiny watch him. Obviously, you two can't be trusted alone together."

Nora nodded. "I'm sorry. I just..."

She put a hand on her shoulder. "It's okay, honey. Don't worry about it."

"Nora," said Billie. "I'm sorry. I swear to God, I didn't mean to hurt you. I... I'm sorry."

She nodded and looked away.

"Go get Tiny," said Kristie, taking the ax from Nora. "I'll watch him until we get his hands tied again."

"Not so tight this time," said Nora, softly. "His wrists are raw."

"I'll tell Tiny."

Nora left the bedroom, trying not to cry. It was obvious as to what was happening to Billie. He was changing into a zombie and she was going to lose another person she held dear to her heart.

27

"Looks pretty quiet," said Henry as they approached the Mall of America. "Except for all the damage to the building, you wouldn't even know what was happening all around it."

"Yeah, it's quiet; too quiet," I said.

It definitely didn't look like a survivor bunker. Just like every other place that had once been bustling with people prior to the apocalypse, it now appeared more like an abandoned ghost-town, even with all the vehicles still parked outside of the ginormous building.

"Should we park in one of the ramps?" asked Bryce.

"Why?" asked Paige. "Let's just park right outside of Macy's or Sears. I think it's safe to say we're not going to get towed."

"I don't know if I want to park right out in the open," he replied. "I'd rather sneak up on this guy and find out what's going on. Just in case his intentions aren't exactly what he's been spouting over the airwaves."

"I agree," said Henry. "If it's who I think it is, this guy might be pulling in survivors and taking their supplies."

Paige snorted. "Because he doesn't have enough of his own, in one of the world's largest shopping malls?"

"She has a point," I said.

Henry sighed. "Yeah, but I still say it sounds like that Travis character. What do you think, Wild?"

"I really don't know," I said. It *had* kind of sounded like Travis, but I couldn't be certain.

Bryce looked back at me. "Regardless, we all still have to be on guard. Don't forget what happened in Atlanta. You just can't trust anyone."

"Yeah," said Henry. "I agree with Bryce. We'd better park somewhere inconspicuous. Pull into a ramp."

We pulled into the east ramp, and ended up parking next to several other vehicles on the first floor.

"Hey," said Bryce, as he got out of the van. "I don't think these are abandoned cars."

Henry touched the top of the Honda parked next to us. "This one is still pretty warm. Like they just got here themselves."

"Let's go," said Bryce. "See if we can find whoever arrived in these cars."

"Lead the way," said Henry. "And if you see one of those fancy little electric chairs, grab one. My back is starting to hurt again."

"I'm sure we'll find you something," I said.

We followed Bryce into the stairwell and to the first floor of the mall where it was dark and quiet.

"I guess they haven't established a welcoming committee yet," whispered Paige.

"Guess not," I said, walking next to her. "Man, I forgot how large this place is. It seems even bigger now that we're the only ones inside."

With over five hundred shops and millions of square feet, the mall was like its own little city. With enough security, it was an ideal place for a shelter, which reminded me – where *were* all the zombies?

"Well," sighed Henry. "If this is supposed to be a shelter or bunker of some sort, where the hell is everyone?"

"Exactly," said Bryce as we turned another corner. "Another thing that's pretty strange is, we haven't come across any zombies. Not even a few stragglers."

"That's what I was wondering," I said. "There weren't any outside, either."

"I don't like this," muttered Henry. "Not one bit."

"Hey," I whispered. "You hear that?"

Someone was whistling.

"Hello!" hollered Paige, walking to one of the entrances leading to Nickelodeon Universe.

"Nice," said Bryce, shaking his head angrily. "So much for remaining *inconspicuous*."

The whistling stopped and someone called out, "Hello?!"

"There he is," said Paige, pointing to a lone figure walking toward them through the amusement park. "Hey! Over here!"

The guy, an athletic-looking blonde dressed in crisp black jeans and a blue polo shirt, raised his hand in greeting and then began walking toward us.

"Meow," whispered Paige. "Who'd have thought the mall would still be a place to meet hot guys?"

I smiled, although it bothered me that his clothing did not match his style, which reminded me more of a biker with and outgrown mohawk and piercings. Something definitely wasn't jiving with this guy.

"Welcome," said the man.

"Hey there, young feller," said Henry. "Are you part of the shelter team?"

"Please, follow me," he replied, walking away.

I looked at Paige, who shrugged.

"Okay, since he's hot, we can excuse his weirdness," she whispered.

"Excuse me," called Bryce.

The stranger kept walking.

"Dude, stop for a second!" hollered Bryce.

The man froze and turned around.

Bryce walked up to him. "Where are you taking us, exactly?"

"To him," he answered in a stoic voice. "The man you seek."

Bryce's eyebrows furrowed. "The man we *seek*?"

The guy's face turned red and he broke out into a sweat. "Yes," he said.

Henry shuffled over to him. "Son, are you okay?"

His lips moved but he couldn't quite seem to answer.

"Oh, my God, is he having a seizure or something?" cried Paige.

"What was that?" asked Henry, pressing a hand on his shoulder. "You trying to say something?"

He opened his mouth. "Huhhh…"

Paige turned to me. "Maybe he's handicapped?" "Autistic or something?"

I looked down at the stranger's hand and noticed he was clutching something so tightly that his knuckles were white.

"What do you have there?" I asked, motioning toward his closed fist.

He glanced down at his hand and then back up at me, the look in his eyes desperate.

"Bryce," I said. "Open up his fist. He might have some kind of weapon or something."

Bryce sighed and then grabbed the guy's wrist.

"Nnnooo…" rasped the guy as Bryce tried uncurling his fingers.

"Cassie," said Paige. "Honestly, what kind of weapon could he have that's small enough to fit in the palm of his hand?"

My eyes met the stranger's, whose expression turned from fear to disbelief. Before I could say anything, he opened his fist.

"Oh, my God," I said, staring at the cross necklace. "That's my sister's!"

The man closed his eyes and fell to his knees. "It's true," he croaked. "Thank God."

Henry shook his head in disgust. "Oh, now he talks."

Bryce grabbed him by the front of the shirt. "Where did you get that?"

He looked at me again. "From Allie, her sister."

***

Travis's face turned red. "Dammit!" he raged, throwing his empty beer bottle at the wall of liquor behind the bar. They were in one of the nightclubs on the upper floor of the mall, waiting for Justice to return.

Kylie and Allie, who were sitting in one of the booths, flinched as he threw a second one, shattering glass all over the bar.

"What's wrong?" asked Dwayne, rushing into the restaurant.

"He broke free!" raged Travis. "I can't control him anymore."

"How?"

"He must be one of those 'Born Agains'," he sneered. "Gee, I wonder how that happened?"

Allie looked away.

"Why do we even need him anymore?"

He paused, and then smiled, his entire demeanor changing. "You're right, we don't. We have the girls and they're going to help us locate the baby. Now, go and kill them. Kill them all."

Dwayne bowed and then walked back out of the bar.

The girls stared at each other in horror.

"No," begged Allie, turning to Travis. "Please don't let him kill Justice!"

"Child, not only is he going to slit your friend's throat," chuckled Travis, as he grabbed a warm beer from the cooler. "But he's also going to kill your sisters, and eventually, *every* person that you care about. Damn," he groaned, after taking a long swig of beer. "This is tasty."

"What do you mean?" asked Kylie, standing up. "Do you know where our sisters are?"

Travis sat down at a table across from them and put his feet up. "Why, yes I do," he said, his eyes turning red. "Now, sit back down before I kill Allie, just for shits and giggles. I really only need one of you."

Kylie immediately sat down.

"Now," he said, tapping his fingers on the table. "There's been a change of plans. After I finish this beer, we're going to take ourselves a little ride."

"Where?" asked Kylie, trying not to cry.

He took another pull of his beer and belched. "Cheer up. I'm going to bring you back to your mommy."

28

"Excuse me?" I gasped.

"He has your sister and Kylie," said Justice.

"I think she means the part of him being some kind of demon. You know, an *entity* from Hell," said Paige with a smirk.

"I know you guys think I'm crazy, hell, I would too if I hadn't seen the stuff he can do with my own eyes. He actually took possession of my body, for God's sake."

I tried not to smile. "And, how'd you get it back?" I asked, wondering if he was a complete nut-job.

He nodded toward the necklace I was holding. "I think it had something to do with that," he smiled sheepishly, "and the fact that I finally believe in God."

"You didn't before?" asked Bryce.

He sighed. "No. Not until today."

"So, you say this guy's name is really Travis?" asked Henry.

"That's what he claims, but I'm sure it's not his real name."

"See, Wild," said Henry. "I told you it was that pecker-head, didn't I?"

"Yeah you did. So," I said, turning back to Justice. "I think it's time you took us to my sister and Kylie."

Before he could answer, the sound of gunfire exploded all around us and we all crouched down on our hands and knees.

"Cassie!" hollered Bryce, grabbing my hand and pulling me with him. "Come on, this way!"

"Paige!" I screamed, looking back for her.

"I'm fine!" she hollered. She was kneeling behind a large garbage can with Justice crouched down beside her.

We scurried over to the other side of the level to a purse kiosk and Bryce pointed. "There."

I looked up and saw Dwayne as he aimed the gun toward us and began firing once again.

"Shit!" growled Bryce, pulling me down.

"What are we going to do?"

"We're going to have to get up there and take him down, because I'm no marksman. There's no way I'll hit him from this distance."

Just then, I looked over at Henry, who was standing up without any kind of cover, had his gun raised, and was aiming for Dwayne.

"What is he doing?" I gasped. "He'll never hit him at that range with a shotgun!"

Bryce swore, then raised his revolver and fired up toward Dwayne.

"Henry!" I screamed, trying to get his attention when Dwayne ducked behind a wall.

Henry lowered his gun and crouched back down.

"I'm going up there," said Bryce, pointing toward the escalators, which were shut down. "You try to distract him somehow."

"How?" I asked.

"I don't know," he pointed to my T-shirt. "Flash him or something."

I scowled. "Very funny."

"It wouldn't work anyway, he wouldn't be able to see much."

I smacked his shoulder. "Bryce!"

"For God's sake, I'm saying he's too far away!"

I stared at him for a second. "Don't you dare smile."

Biting back a grin, he turned and fired, then bolted behind a coffee stand that was closer to the escalators.

"Better give yourselves up!" hollered Dwayne. "You can't beat him. He'll skin you all alive and eat you for dinner if you don't stand down!"

"Cassie!" whispered Paige, loudly. "Look out!"

I looked behind me and saw two zombies approaching the kiosk.

Crap!

It was obvious they weren't there to buy, but I began chucking purses at them anyway.

"Where's your bat?" asked Paige, coming up behind me just as the first zombie rounded the corner.

"I dropped it," I said, as she swung her bat and bashed the zombie's skull in.

"Nice going," she snorted, as I raised my leg and kicked the other zombie in the face, sending him flying backwards.

I sighed. "I know, not very smart. Crap, here comes another one."

The third zombie charged us but was stopped when Justice slammed a metal chair into his face. When the creature stood back up, he quickly grabbed a long metal paper hole-punch that was sitting on the kiosk, and drove it into the zombie's skull.

Paige nodded in approval, and when he turned away, I noticed her checking out his buns.

I smiled.

If we got out of this alive, it was my turn to tease the crap out of *her*.

"Where's Bryce?" she asked.

"He went up the escalator," said Justice.

I looked up but couldn't see Bryce or Dwayne, nor did I hear any more gunfire.

"Henry!" I whispered loudly.

He was still hiding in the same spot, and when he turned, I could see that he'd just stuck another wad of chew into his mouth.

"What?" he hollered.

"Where'd Bryce go?"

Before he could respond, we heard gunfire from above. This time it was deeper in the mall.

I stood up and began moving toward the escalator. They'd obviously moved and there was no way I was going to stay down here if Bryce needed me.

Plus, he only had so many rounds.

"No!" hollered Henry. "Wild, you get your ass back to that kiosk!"

Ignoring him, I ran as fast as I could up the escalator and then hid behind another garbage container.

"What are you doing?" whispered Justice, who'd obviously followed me.

"Bryce is going to need my help," I whispered back.

Another round of gunfire and my stomach started twisting into knots.

If anything happened to Bryce…

"Sorry, but you're no help without a gun," said Justice.

"You haven't seen me in action," I replied, and then ran toward another kiosk, this one a calendar shop.

"Well, look who we have here?" chuckled Dwayne, popping his head around the side of the booth.

My heart sank as he raised the gun and pointed it at my face. "It's a shame, sweetheart. I really thought you and I could have had ourselves a good time the other day."

"Wait," I squeaked, raising my hands slowly to my waist. I un-tucked my shirt.

He chuckled. "What are you doing, brown eyes? Changed your mind?"

Holding my breath, I lifted my T-shirt up and flashed him.

His eyes widened but before he could say anything, I heard a loud blast and he fell forward.

"You're supposed to show all the goods when you flash someone, Wild," said Henry, his gun still smoking. "Not just that little training bra."

My face turned bright pink and I pulled my shirt back down right before Bryce arrived.

"Everyone okay?" he asked, out of breath.

"Not everyone," said Henry, spitting his chew on the dead man's back. "Looks like he got more than he was expecting with Wild here."

Bryce put his arm around my shoulders. "You okay?"

I nodded.

Henry smiled. "Bryce, what were *you* doing when she was whipping out those headlights of hers?"

"I was cornered by a couple of zombies," answered Bryce. "What in the hell are you talking about? What headlights?"

"Nothing," I said, shooting Henry a dirty look. "Look, we need to find Allie and Kylie. Justice!"

"Right here," he said, walking toward us with Paige.

"Where are they?" I asked.

He looked up toward the top floor. "If they're still here, that's where they'd be."

"What do you mean, still here?" I asked.

"He's using the girls to find the baby," said Justice.

"What baby?" asked Paige.

"He called him 'The Chosen One'."

"Whatever," said Bryce. "This Travis sounds like a real fruit-loop. Let's go look for the girls."

"One thing," said Justice, halting him. "This guy has powers – some kind of supernatural ones. Don't underestimate him, and don't let him touch you."

"I don't intend to," said Bryce, moving around him toward the escalators.

"Neither did I," replied Justice, rushing after him.

"He ain't touchin' me, neither," said Henry. "No siree... I don't go for any of that flim-flam stuff."

"Flim-flam?" asked Paige.

He adjusted his hat. "Yeah, you know... the freaky-deaky kind that usually happens in the 'john' at one of those rainbow bars. Hell, you go in to take a dump, and the noise in the next stall isn't from someone pushing one out, it's from someone pushing one in."

I groaned.

"You're a sick man, Henry," mumbled Paige.

"Why, 'cause I tell it like it is?" He lifted the shotgun and waved it toward the escalators. "Come on now, let's go take care of business."

29

Travis ushered the girls across the mall and down one of the emergency stairwells when the gunfire began.

"You try anything," he'd warned before they'd left the club, "I'll burn your flesh from the bone while you're still breathing." Then he raised his hand and a small ball of fire appeared above his fingertips. As they stared at the flames, an image of both girls screaming in agony appeared inside of the fire. He smiled. "I advise you not to test me."

When they stepped outside of Macy's, a dark SUV was waiting for them. The driver, an older man with jet-black hair and glasses, stepped out of the vehicle and held the door open for the girls.

"Get in," demanded Travis, when they hesitated.

Both girls glanced back toward the mall entrance and then their eyes met.

Help was so close.

"Don't even think about trying to escape," warned Travis, forming another ball of fire. He rolled it in his hands until it grew larger and then flung it at a small group of zombies shuffling toward them. The flames consumed them, although they kept moving. It wasn't until Travis whispered something that the zombies halted and continued to burn until they were just piles of ash. "You see, girls, the fires of Hell are hotter than anything up here," he said with a nod of approval. He turned back to the girls. "Now, get in before you find out just how hot."

The girls quickly got into the backseat and Travis slipped in front with the driver.

"Where to?" asked the short little man.

Travis smiled darkly. "Over the river and through the woods, to grandmother's house we go."

***

"They've already left," said Justice, staring at the empty beer bottles left on the bar. "This is the last place that I saw him with your sisters."

"Where do you think they went?" asked Bryce.

"I have no idea," said Justice.

"Isn't it obvious?" I said. "He's looking for a baby."

"Adria," mumbled Paige.

"He's looking for a baby boy," said Justice.

"Maybe he's changed his mind," said Henry.

Bryce sighed. "Guys, how would he even know about Adria?"

"In a simple world, he wouldn't," I said. "But things are happening – crazy, totally unpredictable things that we obviously can't explain."

Henry cleared his throat. "I agree. You know me – I'm older than dirt, stubborn as a mule, and very much set in my ways. But even I have to admit, there's some strange stuff happening and we can't always go with what's rational."

"Let's head back to my grandparents' house," I said. "Maybe we'll get lucky and find them there."

***

NORA

Nora sat on the porch, rocking, as she stared blindly toward the street. Memories, both good and bad, of her childhood flitted through her mind, mostly of the times she'd spent with her grandmother when she was little and her father was on the road.

As a child, she'd never noticed that Grams had been different, or her father, for that matter. To her, she'd always been the smiling, robust woman with the bright blue eyes and silvery black hair always tied back in a loose bun. The kind and loving woman whom she used to dance and sing with, the person who had always encouraged her to speak her mind and not let anyone push her around. She'd tried teaching her the importance of being independent and brave, and to live life without regret. Unfortunately, Grams had preached it, but had never been able to follow her own advice. She'd kept that from Nora, and it wasn't until she'd started school that she'd first glimpsed her grandmother's phobia of the world outside. Sadly, now everyone had to fear the world outside and the nightmares walking the streets, both during the day and night. It was as if Grams had known these days would come.

Thunder rumbled above and Nora leaned forward, wiping away stray tears. Being a pansy wasn't going to help her bring her family back, and it certainly wasn't going to do anything for Billie, either.

Sighing, she stood up and turned toward the door when the sound of an engine caught her attention.

A Suburban.

It slowed and then came to a complete stop in front of the house, just as the rain started.

She ignored the drops and walked toward the vehicle with her hand on the ax. When the back door opened up and she saw the familiar face, she sighed in relief.

"Allie! Oh, my God, we've been looking all over for you. Is Kylie with you?"

Allie nodded and then both girls slid out of the back.

"Who's with you?" asked Nora, trying to catch a glimpse of the two people in front. The windows were so dark, she could barely see their silhouettes.

Neither girl said anything, just stared at her with fear in their eyes.

Not good.

"Um, why don't you girls run into the house and I'll just thank your ride personally."

Just then, the front passenger door opened up and the dirt-bag, Travis, stepped out of the SUV.

"Well, well, well… we meet again," he laughed. "How delightful. Well, I'll bet you didn't expect this happy reunion when you woke up this morning."

"Get into the house, girls," said Nora, raising her voice. "Now!"

"Tsk, tsk," said Travis, walking up to her as the girls started running toward the porch. "I don't know about you, but I don't think that's the right way to greet someone who has just returned your friends."

"You asshole," she growled, raising her ax. "Get the hell out of here or I'll chop off one of your hands and make sure you never start another fire as long as you live."

"Oh, scary," he giggled, mocking her with his hands waving in the air.

"You should be scared, you prick."

His smile fell. "You're beginning to bore me, girl and my time is valuable. I think it's time for you to meet your maker, unless he's given up on your pathetic soul."

Her rage got the best of her. Just when she was about to take a swing, the sound of groans and snarls caught their attention and they both turned toward the street.

"Oh, my God," she gasped in horror.

Hundreds of zombies had turned the corner of the street and were moving toward them through the pouring rain.

Travis smiled and clapped his hands. "Ah… some of my lovely minions have arrived to assist me. Oh, this is going to be fun to watch."

Nora turned and ran to the front door when Tiny opened it from the inside.

"What's happening?" he asked, taking a step outside. "Who's that guy?"

"He's not what he appears." She pointed toward the zombies. "And check that out, we've got some major problems."

He swore and then turned around. "Kristie! Get my gun!"

"Oh, you're going to need more than that," chuckled Travis, stepping onto the porch.

Furious, Nora turned around and launched herself at Travis.

"Foolish mortal," he growled, catching her by the throat. "You just don't learn, do you?"

Nora's face turned red as he lifted her into the air and flung her down the steps and onto the grass.

Stunned, Tiny rushed Travis, but found himself slammed back into the door with such force, that he slid down to his butt.

"What in the hell is going on out here?!" hollered Kristie, now standing over him by the doorway. "Oh, my God, Nora, are you okay?" She looked down at Tiny. "What the hell are you doing, Tiny? Your jeans are getting soaked."

"Get in the house, Kristie," he replied hoarsely.

Nora stood up and grabbed her ax. "That's it. I'm not playing nice anymore. You're going down, freak."

"You can't hurt me, girl," scoffed Travis. "Look, people, just give me the infant and this will all go away."

Tiny stood up and grabbed the gun out of Kristie's hands. "That's it, brother, get the hell off of this property or I'll shoot your ass to the curb."

Travis smiled. "Tell you what – I will leave and even take my army with me if you give up the child."

Kristie and Tiny stared at each other and then at the large crowd of zombies that were nearing the edge of the grass.

Kristie looked at Travis. "Your *army*?"

He turned toward the zombies and shrugged. "Yeah, I know, they aren't exactly the most pristine of soldiers, but they're all I have at the moment."

Tiny raised the gun. "Listen, I don't know what the hell is going on here, but you'd better turn it around and get back into that SUV."

Travis sighed. "Very well. I guess we're going to have to do things the messy way. No worries, though. I always enjoy watching other people's blood being spilled."

"From where I'm standing, it looks like yours is the only one that's going to be spilled," said Tiny, cocking the gun. "Now, move it."

"Tiny, with your determination and biceps, I'm quite certain that you'd make an impressive assistant, since the position appears to be open again. Tell me," he wrinkled his nose, "Are you a noble man?"

"Damn straight."

"So I take it you're a Christian? A believer?"

"Of God? Certainly. Just like I believe you're going to be meeting him very soon if you don't get your ass off of this porch."

"Pity. Well," he said, turning around and lifting his hand in the air. "Let the bloodshed commence!"

The zombies, who'd been eerily waiting on the street, lurched forward toward the house.

30

"Lord Almighty, would you look at that?!" gasped Henry as we turned the corner to my grandparents' street. Hundreds of zombies were gathered around the house, trying to get in, and there was a black SUV parked in front of the house.

"That guy is definitely after Adria," I said, holding on to the seat as Bryce whipped around the block to the back alley.

"We have to get them out of that house before they find a way in," said Henry. "There's too many zombies."

We pulled up to the garage and all of us jumped out of the van clutching our weapons.

"Here," said Bryce, tossing Justice a wrench. "You're going to need it."

"Thanks."

I threw open the gate by the garage, ran down the concrete steps with Paige, and rushed to the back door just as the zombies broke through the side gate.

"Wild!" hollered Bryce. "Get into the house!"

The back door was locked and I began pounding on it. "Kristie! Tiny!"

"Get back, you creeps!" yelled Paige, swinging her bat at the zombies barreling toward us. As the metal hit pay-dirt, I could hear Bryce and Henry emptying their shotguns into the crowd of dead.

"Oh, thank God!" cried Kristie, swinging the door open.

"Stand back, girls!" hollered Tiny as he ran past us with an iron fireplace poker toward the zombies.

"We have to get Adria out of here," I said to Kristie as she pulled me and Paige into the kitchen.

"I know," she said. "There's a crazy lunatic out front who wants to take her away."

I looked past Kristie at Nora, who held Adria in her arms. "Is it Travis?"

"It sure is. Don't worry," said Nora. "There is no way in *hell* that I'm letting that monster have Adria."

More gunshots from outside.

"I have to get back out there and help kill those zombies," I said. "You guys get the baby ready for travel. Something tells me we don't have a lot of time."

"Cassie!"

I turned to find my sister running toward me. She flung herself into my arms and I squeezed her tightly.

"What were you thinking?" I said, blinking back tears. "We could have lost you! Where's Kylie?"

"Right here," said Kylie, stepping into the kitchen with a bag. "I grabbed some diapers and things for Adria."

"Hi, Kylie," said Paige, giving her a quick hug. "You okay?"

She nodded. "Yeah, now that we're with you guys. Mom, we have to leave before that demon takes Adria away."

Kristie sighed. "He's not a demon." She looked at me. "She keeps insisting that weirdo outside is some kind of demon."

I bit my lower lip. "Actually, I'm starting to think he is, too."

She looked at me like I was insane. "What?"

"They're right, mom. I mean, seriously, you wouldn't believe the things that we've seen and heard about him. Evidently, Travis, this demon or whatever he is, believes that Adria might be the 'Chosen One'," said Paige.

"The 'Chosen One'? Chosen for what?" asked Kristie, walking over to the baby.

"Chosen to save the world," replied Kylie, stepping closer to Nora. "The one who's going to defeat Satan and save our souls."

Adria grinned as if she knew what we were talking about and we all stared at her.

Kristie cleared her throat. "Um –"

Just then, we heard a loud crash from the front of the house.

"Oh, my God, the zombies have already gotten in!" hollered Paige.

"Oh, my God!" mimicked Travis, walking through the kitchen door. "Whatever will we do?!"

The baby stared at him, her lip began to tremble, and then she started to wail.

"Out, Demon!" hollered Kristie, crossing her fingers together to form a "T".

"Seriously?" cried Travis, roaring with laughter.

"Get Adria out the back, quickly!" I yelled to Nora.

"Wow, would you look at this," said Travis, staring at all of us. "I'm kind of outnumbered here by women. I think we'd better remedy this situation."

He then snapped his fingers and Billie, who was no longer restrained, stumbled through the kitchen door.

"Billie!" cried Nora, reaching one of her hands toward him.

He didn't answer.

I stared at my new friend in horror, realizing that something was very wrong. Earlier today he'd been slightly pale but now his face was ashen, his eyes unfocused.

"Grab the child," ordered Travis.

Billie lurched toward Nora and we all tried blocking his path.

"Stop it, Billie!" I yelled, trying to push him back.

He growled and began snapping his teeth at me.

"Oh hell, just destroy them," demanded the demon.

I stared into Billie's eyes in horror and realized that he was truly gone. Nothing remained but the zombie who'd taken over his body.

"No!" cried Nora, noticing it too. The despair in her face broke my heart.

"Nora, get Adria out of here!" I cried, as Kristie and I tried holding Billie's face away from my skin. "The girls, too!"

With a choked sob, Nora ran through the back of the house, followed by Kylie and Allie.

"That's it," growled Travis. "Finish these three and meet me out back."

"I don't think so," snarled Henry, stepping through the kitchen, his shotgun raised. "You ain't meeting nobody but your friends in Hell, *Slick*."

Then he fired the gun, hitting Travis in the middle of his chest.

We all screamed as Travis fell backwards, a large bloody hole in the middle of his chest. When he hit the tile, his eyes stared lifelessly toward the refrigerator and he didn't move.

"No way," whispered Paige as we stared in disbelief. "Seriously, it can't be that easy?"

I'm not sure what I expected, but it wasn't the dead body of a demon lying in the middle of my grandparents' kitchen.

Billie released my arm and dropped quickly to the ground. I kneeled next to him.

"Is he okay?" asked Kristie, bending down.

"Uh, I think he may have died from the zombie virus," I said, staring at his closed eyelids.

"Wouldn't he be attacking us right now then?" asked Henry, staring down at us.

I touched Billie's cheek and sucked in my breath. "Oh, my God, he's still warm. And look, the color is coming back to his cheeks!"

Kristie touched his forehead. "Maybe he's going to be all right?"

Before I could answer, Billie's eyelids began to flutter.

"Billie?" I said, reaching for his hand. "Hey, are you okay?"

His eyes opened. "I'm... back," he whispered staring at me in wonder. "I didn't think it was possible."

I smiled at him in relief. "I guess anything is possible."

He swallowed. "Help me up?"

I stood and pulled him with me. "How are you feeling?"

He touched his cheeks and then smiled broadly. "You know what? I'm doing pretty good actually. I feel great!"

I stared at him in disbelief. He *did* look healthy and refreshed. Nothing compared to the monster who'd tried attacking us. I began to wonder if Travis's death had been the cure for the zombie plague. It certainly didn't seem logical. But then again, nothing I'd seen in the last few weeks seemed real or logical. "You *sure* you're okay?"

"Oh, yeah." He walked to Travis's body and nodded. "Looks like someone did a number on that guy."

"You don't remember anything?" asked Kristie.

"Nope."

"You're lucky," I said.

Our eyes met and he smiled. "Very."

"You must have been in some kind of trance or something," said Henry. "Just like that young man, Justice. Listen, we'd better get out of here and head back to Atlanta. Got us so many dead bodies on the lawn, your neighbors are going to start talking."

"Oh, my God," I said, forgetting all about the zombies in the yard. "How are Bryce and the others doing?"

"They were holding their own, last time I checked," said Henry. "Ordered me into the house to check on you women. Good thing I came when I did."

"I'm going out there," I said.

"No, I'll check," said Henry.

Before I could argue, Bryce barreled through the door looking upset. "Cassie, thank God," he said, pulling me into his arms. "I heard from Nora that Travis made it into the house and I thought I'd lost you."

"He did make it in here but Henry took care of him," I replied, closing my eyes.

"Yep," said Henry. "Shot that sucker straight through the heart."

"See, what did I tell you?" said Bryce, releasing me.

I arched my eyebrow. "Tell me?"

He walked over to Travis's dead body, and with a grimace, said, "There's no way this guy was a demon. If he was, he'd still be alive."

"That's what I thought," said Kristie, clucking her tongue. "You girls and your wild imaginations."

I sighed. "I suppose you're right."

"I want to leave," said Paige, looking pale. "All of this blood is making me nauseous."

Kristie put an arm around her. "I hear you."

"I agree," I replied. "Plus, I'm tired and could use a nap."

"Really?" snorted Bryce. "I just took out forty or fifty zombies on my own. If anyone could use a nap, it's me."

"Fine," I said. "I'll drive while you and Adria take your little naps."

Henry cleared his throat. "I don't think that's such a good idea. We all know how you drive."

"Everything okay in here?" asked Nora, walking back into the house with Tiny.

"Check it out," said Paige. "We killed the demon!"

Nora stared at Billie in disbelief. "Billie? Oh, my God, are you okay?"

He smiled and raised his arms. "I'm doing great."

She rushed over and threw her arms around him. "Thank God," she mumbled. "I thought I'd lost you."

He chuckled. "You can't lose me that easily."

"Where's Adria?" asked Kristie.

"She's fine. She's in the van with the girls," said Nora, still staring up at Billie in wonder. "Sorry, but I still can't get over this."

He kissed her on the forehead. "I know. I'm not an easy guy to take down."

"Good thing," she said, releasing him.

Kristie turned to Tiny. "Did you guys take care of all the zombies?"

"We got most of them. There are still some heading this way, but nothing we can't handle," he replied.

"What about Travis's driver?" she asked. "Are we going to have a problem with him, too?"

"Nah, he took off," said Tiny. "When I tried approaching him, he flew down the street like a bat out of hell."

She smiled. "I'll bet."

"I can't believe everyone made it," I said, staring at everyone. After the last few hours, it seemed like a miracle.

"Everyone but Luke," sighed Kristie, shaking her head somberly. "Poor kid,"

Bryce's face fell. "Yeah, that poor kid. Justice told me what happened. I still can't believe it."

"Belinda's going to be devastated," said Henry, scratching his whiskers. "Even if they weren't really related. She grew quite attached to that kid."

None of us said anything. We'd all lost so many loved ones in the last few weeks and it never got easier. If anything, Luke's death was a reminder that none of us were safe from the threats still out there. All threats. Whether our enemies were zombies or people, we had to watch our backs very carefully.

"Well, we should get going," said Billie.

We agreed and started packing up what was left of the snacks, water, and baby supplies.

"I should make the baby a bottle for the road," said Kristie.

"Good idea," said Tiny, handing her the canister of formula and a bottle of water.

"Everything ready?" asked Bryce, carrying a couple of extra pillows from the bedroom.

"We just have to load the vehicles."

Billie walked over to Kristie. "Why don't I bring the bottle to the girls and let them start feeding Adria."

She handed it to him. "Sounds good. We'll be right out."

"Okay," he said, walking out the back door. "Take your time so you don't forget anything."

"So, who are you riding with, Justice?" asked Paige.

He shrugged. "I don't know. You guys okay with me tagging along?"

Paige twirled her blond hair around her finger, and stared at him as if he was the last pair of

Jimmy Choos on the face of the Earth and she couldn't live without them. "Uh, of course you have to come with. You're part of the team now."

He smiled. "Then, I guess I'll be riding with whoever wants me."

"Of for crying out loud, you'll be riding with Paige," said Henry, getting up from the kitchen table. "That girl has had her knickers in a bundle ever since she's laid eyes on you."

Paige's face turned crimson. "Don't listen to him. He doesn't know what he's talking about."

Justice's lip twitched. "Too bad. I always wanted to know what knickers in a bundle looked like."

"Hey, that's my daughter you're flirting with over there, young man," said Kristie. "There will be no knickers bundling up anywhere. Period."

"Really, mom," mumbled Paige, walking out of the kitchen.

"Oh, I think you're in for an earful later, Kristie," I giggled.

She shrugged. "That's fine. I'm used to it."

I laughed and went outside to join Paige.

"Cassie!" hollered Paige, standing on the side of the garage. "I don't see the van. Did the guys move it to the front of the house?"

"Not that I know of," I said, walking up the cement steps.

Sure enough, the van was nowhere to be found.

It was missing.

Her face turned white. "I think we have another problem on our hands."

***

"You girls doing okay back there?" asked Billie, as he turned the van onto the freeway.

"Yeah," said Kylie, closing her eyes, trying to block out the sounds of Adria's cries.

"I don't know what's wrong with her. She just finished her bottle," said Allie. "So she can't be hungry. Poor thing."

"Well, we have a long way to go before we reach our destination. You need to try and shut her up," replied Billie.

"That's not nice," said Kylie, opening her eyes. "She can't help it, you know, she's just a little baby."

"I don't care; keep her quiet so I can concentrate on the road."

"Um, so you never told us, why are we riding with you and not the others?" asked Kylie.

He looked back at her in the rearview mirror but didn't say anything.

The hair on the back of Kylie's neck stood straight up. "Billie?"

A cold, evil smile spread across his handsome face. "I prefer that you call me... Travis."

***

END OF BOOK FOUR

Ready for the conclusion?

Now Available!

As a cold darkness settles upon the world, our heroes search frantically for their friends and family. Meanwhile, two evils come together and try to destroy the child they believe to be the true "Chosen One". Will they succeed and annihilate all of mankind?

agrees to visit his family's new shop, Secrets, and is